heart of flames

BOOK THREE

VAMPIRE ROYALS OF NEW YORK

Heart of Flames
Vampire Royals of New York: Gabriel
Book Three
Copyright © 2021 by Sarah Piper
SarahPiperBooks.com

Cover design by Covers by Juan

ISBN-13: 978-1-948455-27-5

ALSO BY SARAH PIPER

VAMPIRE ROYALS OF NEW YORK

Dorian

Dark Deception

Dark Seduction

Dark Obsession

Gabriel

Heart of Thorns

Heart of Fury

Heart of Flames

TAROT ACADEMY

Spells of Iron and Bone

Spells of Breath and Blade

Spells of Flame and Fury

Spells of Blood and Sorrow

Spells of Mist and Spirit

THE WITCH'S REBELS

Shadow Kissed

Darkness Bound

Demon Sworn

Blood Cursed

Death Untold

Rebel Reborn

THE WITCH'S MONSTERS

Blood and Midnight

CHAPTER ONE

Renault Duchanes would *burn* for this.

Gabriel could scarcely see through the haze of his red-hot fury. His hand trembled, the phone clutched inside it seconds from cracking.

"You've just signed your death warrant, bloodsucker," he warned, but the line had already gone dead. Duchanes had made his singular demand—hand over the witch, or the wolf dies—and that was that.

They had until dawn to comply. And in the scant few hours remaining, Gabriel was certain Cole would endure the kind of torture that would make hell look like an amusement park.

Fuck.

Gabriel closed his eyes, trying to focus.

Plan. He needed a fucking plan. But even if Duchanes *hadn't* warned them to come alone, they were out in the middle of the woods, hours away from anyone who could've helped. With Cole's life already in mortal danger, Gabriel wasn't about to put Dorian, Aiden, Colin, or Isabelle in the line of fire.

Beyond that, there was no one else he trusted to outmaneuver Duchanes, rescue the wolf, and keep his woman safe.

Gabriel sighed. In this, he and his witch were utterly on their own, which meant it would all come down to him. He didn't give a fuck *what* Duchanes had demanded—Jacinda wasn't getting anywhere near the bastard.

For a moment, the world fell silent, the only sounds the frantic pounding of his heart and the echo of Duchanes' threats.

I want my witch returned to me…

The thought of that wretched vampire putting his hands on Jacinda, using her, tormenting her, feeding from her…

The phone exploded in his hand.

By the time Gabriel saw the blood and felt the sharp bite of broken glass and metal, the wounds were already healing.

If only he could say the same for his heart.

"Gabriel," a soft voice broke through the tempest of his thoughts. Almost a whisper. Almost a prayer.

Jacinda…

The lightest touch of her hand against his face brought him back from the precipice.

His vision finally cleared.

His rage, however, did not.

If anything, looking into her bright blue gaze only further stoked the flames.

"It's okay," Jacinda said gently. "We'll figure this out."

"Nothing to figure out. I told you I'd destroy anyone who dared to touch you, did I not?"

The faintest smile lit up her face, and she slid her hands behind his neck, her warm body pressed firmly against his. "Actually, you said you'd bleed and burn them. Monster, man, or mage."

"Brilliant. That's precisely what I'll do, then. In that order." He brushed a quick kiss across her mouth. The contact was all-too-brief, but if Gabriel lingered so much as another *minute* over those soft lips, the courage to walk out that door would surely abandon him. "I'll call you when it's done."

She glanced down at the shattered phone still gripped in his hand. "Right. And while you're off vanquishing the enemy, I'm supposed to just, what? Netflix and chill with my knockoff Irish coffee?"

"Yes." He turned away from her to hunt down his clothes. He found them on the floor, half-buried by the comforter he and Jacinda had been wrapped up in most of the night, and quickly changed. "I'll find a way to get in touch. Just… just lock the doors and windows and lie low until I or one of my brothers comes back for you."

Ignoring his protests, Jacinda retrieved her clothes from the floor, tugging on the jeans she'd worn earlier. Dirt from the Enchanted Gardens still clung to the bottoms, a stark reminder of their passionate tumble beneath the rose bushes that stirred Gabriel's cock to rapt attention.

But when he met her gaze again, it wasn't lust he found there.

Only anger.

"So that's the whole plan?" she said, hands on her hips, wild curls damn near crackling with the sudden force of her emotion. "Storm the castle, bleed and burn the bad guys, save the wolf?"

"Clear and concise. Less room for error that way."

"Less room for success too."

"It *will* work, Jacinda. It has to."

"You've left out a few crucial steps, Prince."

"Such as?"

"How are you going to capture Duchanes and save Cole?"

"I'm not going to capture Duchanes. I'm going to eviscerate him. Wait, no—bleed and burn him. That's what I said. Even better."

"We need him alive, Gabriel. He's our only shot at breaking the curse."

"The curse is the least of my worries tonight."

"Not mine."

"Jacinda, we don't have time to argue about this. I need to—"

"How are we supposed to get past the security guys, anyway? Cole said the warehouse is—"

"*We're* not getting past anyone." Gabriel shoved his feet into his boots and grabbed his jacket, wishing like hell he could trade it all for the comforter instead, spend the rest of the night before the fireplace in a storm of hot, sweaty limbs and feverish kisses and…

No. He needed to lock Jacinda inside, secure the cabin, and make for Newark. The sooner he could reach Duchanes, the sooner he could end this nightmare.

The sooner he could get back to his woman.

"This is a solo mission, Jace," he said firmly. "And if I've got any hope of saving the wolf, I need to leave now."

"Has anyone ever told you you're *super* adorable when you're full of shit?" She shot him a condescending smile, then dropped it, her face turning stone-cold serious. "Go shovel the driveway so we can get the car out of here. I'll put on the coffee."

"Jacinda, I told you. You're staying in this cabin until—"

"If you so much as *think* about leaving without me, I'm never talking to you again. Or kissing you. Or doing that thing with my tongue and the—"

In a flash he had her pinned against the wall, hands fisting her hair, mouth close to her ear. "Do *not* disobey me on this, little moonflower. Your protests, however valiant, are pointless. You're staying here. End of discussion. Understood?"

"Fuck off, Prince." She shoved against his chest, glaring up at him with new fire in her eyes. "I'm coming whether you like it or not. Your only choice is whether I ride shotgun with you or strap on a pair of snowshoes and make for the highway. Maybe some trucker will take pity and offer me a lift."

Gabriel tightened his fist in her hair, trying to fight off the urge to kiss her. How the fuck could he be so enraged and so turned on at the same time?

"You wouldn't dare," he warned.

"Try me, dickhead."

Heat rose between them, a whiff of hellfire scenting the air. A low, possessive growl rumbled through Gabriel's chest, but Jacinda refused to back down.

"What's it going to be, vampire?" she asked. "Am I riding with you, or taking my chances with that trucker?"

"You're bloody *impossible*, witch."

"Nope. Just determined."

"Determined to get yourself killed?" Gabriel finally released her and paced the room, red haze clouding his vision once more. "Are you mad? For fuck's sake, woman. As much as I love talking to you, and kissing you, and *especially* that thing you do with your tongue, I'd give it all up in a heartbeat for a chance to keep you safe. Don't you get that?"

"Doesn't matter. Renault said—"

"It's a trap, Jacinda. The moment we set foot in that warehouse, he'll take you from me, and I can't—"

"Of course he'll take me! That's the deal—me for Cole. There are no other options here, Gabriel. If we don't give him what he wants—or at least make it *look* like we're giving him what he wants—Cole's dead. And who's next? One of your brothers?"

"Not happening. I'll find Cole and deal with Duchanes before anything—"

"You don't know that. Renault's a smug asshole, but he's not completely stupid. He'll expect a double-cross."

"Doesn't mean he'll be able to defend against it."

"And if he can? What do you think happens to me then?" She grabbed her coat and boots, ignoring his protests. "He knows we're here, Prince. He's obviously got people watching the place. The minute he realizes I'm not with you, I'm dead. And this time, I doubt his goons will do me the courtesy of leaving a decapitated wolf as a warning."

"*Jacinda…*"

Gabriel cursed under his breath.

Fucking hell, she was right. Gabriel knew it—he'd known it as soon as Duchanes had issued the demand. There was no way around this. They either showed up together as ordered, or the dawn would bring nothing but death.

Cole's. Jacinda's. Dorian's. His own.

"Trust me on this," she said, reaching for his hand. "Please, Gabriel."

Gabriel finally stopped pacing and turned to face her again. Slid his hands back into her silky hair. Tried one more time to break through her obstinate, reckless, beautiful audacity—a thing he loved and loathed in equal measure.

"You risked your life to save Charlotte," he said softly. "Now you're ready to do it all over again for Cole?"

"Seriously? How is that even a question?"

"Because it's… You're just… If anything were to… Ah,

moonflower." Gabriel sighed and shook his head. As much as he wanted to chain her to a chair and lock her in the closet to keep her safe, he couldn't help but admire her courage. Her fire. "What happened to the woman ready to sacrifice the whole world just to save her father's soul?"

Tears glazed her eyes, and when she finally answered him, her voice was little more than a sigh. "Maybe she realized she wouldn't be able to look her father in the eyes if she sat on the sidelines and let her friends die."

Gabriel nodded, touched his forehead to hers. There was no use in perpetuating the argument—he'd already lost. "Then let's just be sure we don't let anyone die tonight, shall we?"

"Thanks for the 'we,' Prince."

"We're partners, are we not?" he teased.

"Despite your best efforts to play the lone hero..." She pulled back and grinned, then thrust out her hand. "Hell yeah, we're partners."

Gabriel took it. Held on tight. But he couldn't return her smile—not when he thought about the odds.

"I'm still not sure what the fuck we're doing," he said. "What we're walking into at that warehouse. Duchanes and his vampires? A hundred grays ready to attack? Dark mages preparing for another sacrifice?"

"Whatever it is, we can handle it. Together. We just need three things—well, four, counting the coffee." Jacinda headed to the kitchen.

Gabriel followed, digging out the travel mugs as she set the pot to brew. "And the other three things?"

"A halfway decent plan, a little magic, and your favorite —leverage."

"*Second* favorite." Gabriel slid a hand around the back of her neck, tracing her earlobe with his thumb. "Weapons, Jace. *That's* my first favorite, and you left it off your list entirely. We're not going in there unarmed."

"Silly vampire." She glanced up at him and smirked, her eyes turning demon-black, a hint of silver-blue hellfire flashing through them like an electric current. "Who said anything about going in unarmed?"

CHAPTER TWO

A few hours before dawn, Newark's warehouse district was dark and deserted, no human foolish enough to brave the frigid streets.

Jaci burrowed deeper into her coat and picked her way across a parking lot slick with ice, her breath clouding. The destination was just ahead, a dingy nondescript warehouse that currently served as HQ for Renault and his ragtag army of supernatural freaks.

It'd taken her and Gabriel a while to get there. The snowy mountain roads were a bitch, and they'd had to make a couple of pit stops—a garden center and a spice shop—to procure the ingredients Jaci needed.

And by "procure," she obviously meant "steal," but whatever.

Just add breaking-and-entering to the list of crimes and misdemeanors I'll be repenting for in my eternal hell...

Gabriel had stuffed the registers with cash on their way

out—the only thing marginally easing her guilt about the smash-and-grabs. Well, that and the fact that if they didn't stop Renault tonight, it wouldn't be long before the human world fell into mortal danger too.

Just like Cole.

Cole. Her memories of the wolf shifter—the rough sound of his laughter, the sparkle in his kind eyes, the faint tinge of marijuana that perpetually surrounded him—pushed her onward, every step a lonely echo.

The warehouse loomed large in front of her. No windows, just like Cole had described. No light. No hint as to what was hiding inside those walls.

Gabriel waited in the shadows across the street, cloaked in a spell that temporarily muted his vampire signature from any supernaturals skulking around. Jaci had no idea how things would ultimately go down tonight, but she *did* know this:

If Gabriel accompanied her inside, Renault's goons would surround them in an instant, stake Gabriel into dust, capture Jaci on sight, and shoot the whole half-baked plan to hell.

It'd taken almost the entire drive over for her to convince him of this fact, but eventually, logic won out and he agreed to give her a fifteen-minute head start. Didn't make it any easier to walk away from him now though, knowing the all-too-brief kiss they'd shared in the frigid darkness might just be their last…

No. Hell *no. We just have to get through this shitstorm, then we'll be back in each other's arms, toasting in front of the fire and reminiscing about the time we kicked Renault's ass…*

Sucking in a cold, energizing breath, Jaci hopped up onto a loading dock and made her way toward the two panther shifters guarding the entrance, just as Renault had instructed. Behind them, she could just make out the space inside—a massive concrete room divided by rows of industrial metal shelving, unmarked wooden crates, and steel cages stacked three layers high.

Supernatural creatures of all sorts—little more than science experiments at this point—hissed and cowered inside, rabid and mutilated.

She could only hope Cole wasn't one of them.

Jaci gulped.

Now or never…

"Isn't it a little cold for you boys tonight?" she called out. "Thought panthers preferred the tropics."

They were on her in a flash, one pinning her arms behind her while the other unzipped her coat and gave her a thorough pat-down.

She'd tucked two wooden stakes in her waistband earlier, and he'd found them easily, just like she'd hoped.

"Where's your bloodsucking boyfriend?" The handsy guy felt around to her backside, his searching growing more invasive.

"I was about to ask you the same question," Jaci replied. "Keep digging though—I'm sure he's in there somewhere."

"Don't get cute, witch."

"Can't help it." She shrugged and flashed a smile. "Genetics are a real bitch sometimes, am I right?"

Handsy shot her a glare that could break glass. "Only reason you're still alive is the boss wants it that way. The second he don't, you're ass is mine." As if she needed convincing, he grabbed a handful of her flesh and squeezed. "Now I'll ask again, one more time. Where's Redthorne?"

"Parking the car. Geez." Jaci rolled her eyes. "No valet service here. I'm totally docking a star from my Yelp review."

Handsy glanced at his mute twin, still pinning her arms. "Find him."

The shifter released her and loped down the dock.

He'd be dead in a matter of minutes.

"The fuck you grinnin' about?" Handsy glowered at her, still holding her ass hostage.

Just wondering what a panther looks like wearing his intestines on the outside of his body...

Out loud, she said, "Just wondering if it's true what they say about a man with big hands."

He let out a grunt, a lazy smile stretching across his mouth. "What's that, witch?"

"Big gloves?"

"That's all you got for me?" He squeezed her ass hard enough to leave a bruise. Leaning in close, he growled, "After the boss has his way with you, I'm gonna break you in half."

"Hope you'll at least buy me dinner first."

"Only thing you're eating tonight is dick. Let's go." At this, he finally removed his hand from her backside and gave her a hard shove into the warehouse. Jaci caught herself before she fell, trying to take in as much information as she could—the other exit points, the position of the mages and demons inside, an approximation of just how many enemies they'd be taking on tonight.

The odds were *definitely* not in her favor.

Jaci's confidence faltered. One witch-demon and a royal vampire… against a legion of crazed monsters? Monsters who could very well be juiced up by powers from Viansa?

She almost turned and bolted.

But then Renault Duchanes emerged from the center of the warehouse, sauntering toward her wearing a look of supreme satisfaction, and the fire inside her roared back to life.

You are going down *tonight, motherfucker.*

A few dozen of his buddies loomed behind him—a handful of dark witches she'd seen in his service before, a bunch of mages she hadn't, and a good number of demons and vampires. A few of the vampires held grays on leashes, just like she'd seen that night outside the hospital.

If they decided to attack, she was toast.

Fortunately, Renault didn't like sharing the spotlight *or* calling in backup—liked to make everyone believe he had everything under control at all times. For now, his minions kept their distance, busying themselves by checking the cages, scurrying from one row of shelves to the next, following whatever orders he'd given them.

But Jaci knew the deal. One word from the boss and they'd tear her apart… or worse. Lock her in a cage.

She sucked in another fortifying breath.

Not tonight, fuckers. Not tonight.

Renault took his time getting to her, clearly enjoying the buildup to her so-called surrender.

"You're in deep shit now, blondie," her panther guard whispered, surreptitiously grazing her ass with his palm. "But don't worry—we're still on for later. Sloppy seconds? That's my kink."

Every flame of hellfire inside was screaming to burst free. It roiled in her belly, crackled through her limbs, zipped down her spine until she felt like she might explode with it.

But Jaci didn't flinch. One wrong move and she'd lose this battle before it'd even begun.

Instead, she waited. Thought of the vampire lurking outside in the shadows. Thought of the wolf they were here to rescue. The monsters they were here to end. All the innocent lives they'd save tonight, assuming she stayed calm and everything went as planned.

Renault continued his slow march, king of his concrete castle. But the closer he got, the less kingly he appeared. Despite his posturing, the vampire looked tired and old— much older than she'd remembered. His face was pale and gaunt, dark circles ringing his bloodshot eyes. A faint but noticeable tremor shook his hands.

The curse.

She could almost feel it eating away his life force, one

cell at a time. It was the worst she'd seen of it, and she suspected—left unchecked—it'd probably kill him in a matter of weeks. Days, maybe.

The thought should've filled her with joy. Instead, it terrified her.

The vampire she loved was bound to the same fate.

I will break this, Gabriel. I promise…

"So my witch has finally come to her senses." Renault hummed with pleasure as he approached, his lecherous gaze raking her from head to toe. Stopping just before her, he smiled and said, "Hello, Jacinda. So lovely to see you again."

Jaci lowered her gaze to the floor and hunched her shoulders, a tiny whimper escaping her lips.

Renault hummed again.

Jaci kept her smile at bay.

And the award for Most Convincing Performance in a Vampire Takedown goes to…

"You… you too, Renault," she said softly, forcing a tremble into her voice.

Unlike the panther she'd mouthed off to, her former master required a different approach. One she'd honed over her years of working as his bonded witch, perfecting her technique until the witch she became for *him* was so different from the witch she truly *was*, she no longer recognized herself.

It was Gabriel who'd brought her back. Gabriel who saw the *real* Jacinda hiding inside. The one who fought hard and loved harder, who always spoke her mind, who never let her enemies get the better of her—even the enemy she'd fallen in love with.

Again, her smile threatened to break free.

Again, she buried it.

Renault took a step closer. Fingered a lock of her hair. Licked his greasy lips.

Certain he was close enough to scent her blood, Jaci flipped through her memories of hell, calling up a couple of the most terrifying—she and her father trying to outrun a dozen fanged hellbeasts in the volcanic region of Jenspar. Viansa dousing her in gasoline and locking her in a coffin for three days, flicking lit cigarettes at her until she'd grown bored of the game.

No, it wasn't *true* fear that soured her blood now—just an echo triggered by those dark memories—but the effect would be the same.

She knew it the moment Renault scented it. He perked up immediately. Leaned in close. Dragged his nose along the side of her neck and sniffed as if she were a fine wine.

"Beautiful," he whispered. And this time, Jaci didn't have to fake her shiver. His touch was as repulsive as his face.

"Careful, boss." The handsy panther held up the stakes he'd taken out of her pants. "Bitch was packing."

"Jacinda. Really?" Renault released her hair and drew back. With a quick stomp of his boot, he obliterated the weapons. "And here I thought this was a happy reunion."

"I… I didn't mean… I'm sorry," she stammered, forcing herself to meet his gaze. Calling up a few tears and another bad memory, she dropped her voice to a whisper and said, "I was… I'm… I'm just scared."

Disgust flooded his eyes, but desire quickly followed, just as she'd known it would. Below his beltline, his pants tented out.

He reached for her once more. Brushed his knuckles along her jaw. "You *should* be scared. You know I don't like to be threatened."

Jaci's eyes widened in feigned horror.

Renault smiled again.

The fucker never could resist a damsel in distress.

But unlike her vampire prince, Renault wasn't interested in saving anyone.

Only in dominating. Only in hurting. Only in feeding.

Showtime.

"Please!" Jaci wrapped her arms around her chest and stepped backward, eyes darting everywhere, lip trembling, looking every bit the vulnerable prey Renault wanted to see.

The prey she *needed* him to see.

"I swear," she continued, fake tears rolling down her face. "I swear I wasn't going to stake you, Renault. I'll… I'll do anything you want. Just… please. Please don't hurt me."

"I only hurt those who hurt me, Jacinda." Another grin, a flash of fang, and the monster was on her, hauling her against his chest and sinking his fangs deep into her neck.

Jaci didn't know which was more annoying—the sting of his sloppy bite, or the pencil-dick erection poking her stomach—but she didn't resist him. Just tried to relax as he took his fill.

Slurping. Gulping. Moaning.

Her stomach turned. How she'd managed to live with this pig for so many years without roasting his ass was a damned mystery.

The panther caught her gaze and winked. His pants had tented too.

There was a special word for men who got their kicks overpowering women. A *few* special words, actually. And as the slimy vampire sucked and slurped from her artery, every last one of them raced through her head.

But tonight, in *this* moment, her heart lighter than it'd felt in decades, Jaci had a different word for Renault Duchanes:

Defeated.

CHAPTER THREE

Ten seconds. Fifteen. Thirty.

And away we go…

A new tremor began in Renault's fingers, terrible and obvious, vibrating into Jaci's upper arms where he tried in vain to hold tight. One by one, his fingers loosened, finally releasing her. His fangs slid back into his gums, and he sucked in a rattling breath, then unleashed a bloody cough.

Jaci took a step back, narrowly avoiding the spray. "Something wrong, Renault?"

He reached for her again but missed, stumbling and falling to his knees.

"What the *fuck*?" The asshole panther guard tried to grab her from behind, but Jaci was ready for it. She whirled on him, hitting him head-on with a burst of hellfire.

He was a pile of charred bones before he could even scream.

"Barbecued panther," she said with a satisfied grin. "That's *my* kink, asshole."

Renault coughed again, damn near choking.

"Food allergies?" she asked with a shrug. "You should be more careful about checking the nutrition label before you help yourself to someone's artery."

"You're a… demon?" Renault wheezed. "What… what have you done?"

"Only what you asked me to do. Devise a poison strong enough to kill a vampire? I mean, it didn't actually *kill* Dorian Redthorne, but he's a lot stronger than you." Jaci shrugged and crouched down in front of him. "Should I start taking bets on how long you'll survive? Truth be told, you're not looking so hot, Ren."

"You… you used my poison? On me?"

She cringed and wrinkled her nose. "Is this, like, an intellectual property thing? I never signed an NDA, so I just assumed… Well, damn. This is awkward."

One hand clutching his throat, the other reaching for her, Renault turned the loveliest shade of purple. "Give me… the… antidote."

"I'd love to." Jaci stood up and stretched, letting out a lazy sigh. "But there's only one place in the world the antidote exists, and unfortunately for you, it's not in this warehouse. So if you want to avoid tonight's express train to hell, you should probably do exactly as I say."

Lies. There was no antidote, just like there was no imminent death on Renault's horizon.

The poison she'd crafted tonight was a modified version

of the one she'd made on Renault's orders all those months ago. Unlike its deadlier predecessor, this one was designed to infiltrate Jaci's bloodstream without harming her, but severely weakening any vampire who fed from her.

Left untreated, it probably *would* kill Renault, but not for a few days at least.

Plenty of time to get what they needed from him.

Gabriel had wanted her to kill the vampire outright, but Jaci refused. Not only was the promise of the non-existent antidote their best leverage for getting Cole back, but the vampire's heart was the key to breaking the Redthorne curse. She needed him to stay alive tonight.

Besides, making her former master suffer? That was just fucking fun.

"Where?" Renault panted. "Where is it?"

The other supernaturals had finally sensed the disturbance in the force, and now a few of them were making their way over. Jaci had maybe thirty seconds before they realized their boss was hacking up blood and their security guard was a pile of smoking rubble.

Renault coughed again, trying but failing to get back on his feet. "Filthy mongrel. I… I will—"

"For starters, you'll call off the goon squad, or they'll be sweeping up your ashes by sunrise."

He glared at her and shook his head, but Jaci wasn't about to back down.

She got right in his face, letting her eyes turn black, her palm crackling with fresh hellfire. "Call them off, Renault. *Now*."

With no other options, he held up a hand and shook his head, halting the advancing mob. They'd gotten close, though. Close enough to realize their boss was having a *real* shitty night.

Mages. Vampires. Demons. Grays. Too many to count. Jaci sensed the mages' dark magic on the air, smelled the demons' hellfire. Together they were an arsenal of weapons locked and loaded, every last one ready to blow.

"Stand down," Renault ordered, finally getting to his feet. Pressing a hand to his chest, he cleared his throat and repeated the command. "Stand down."

A murmur of confusion rippled through the group, but eventually, they backed off.

Jaci let out a sigh of relief.

Gabriel would join her soon.

They'd find Cole and get out of there.

The end was so close she could taste it.

Then Renault coughed again and dropped back onto his knees, and *one* vampire—one stupid, inbred, wannabe-hero vampire—decided to break rank.

She'd barely caught sight of his blur before he barreled into her, slamming her to the ground and pinning her beneath two hundred pounds of pure muscle. Jaci couldn't catch her breath. Couldn't fight him off. He fisted her hair, and with a monstrous gleam in his eyes, he bared his fangs, yanked her head to the side, and...

Collapsed in a bloody heap on top of her.

Blinking the gore from her eyes, Jaci looked up as the

face of her rescuer slowly came into focus, one sexy inch at a time.

Chiseled jaw with just the right amount of stubble. Infuriating smirk. Gorgeous green eyes.

In his hand, he clutched the dead vampire's heart.

Seconds later, the heart—along with the rest of the carcass damn near crushing her lungs—exploded in a cloud of ash.

"Honestly, woman." Gabriel dusted off his hands and helped her up. "I'm all for a bit of role-play, but I think you're taking this whole white-knight-saves-damsel thing too far."

"You know I can't resist a good rescue, Prince."

"Speaking of rescues…" He leaned in close, whispering into her hair. "I assume you've got a plan? I mean, you *said* you had a plan, but this… Well, this isn't inspiring much confidence."

Jaci glanced out across the sea of angry, confused faces, all of them clearly waiting for Renault to give the execution order. She could see it in their eyes—the weighing of the options.

Attack now, and risk embarrassing their boss and possibly getting executed for acting without a direct command.

Do nothing, and risk their boss dying before he could line their pockets with whatever riches he'd undoubtedly promised in exchange for their loyalty.

Turn tail and run, hoping like hell he never tracked them down.

Jaci knew the dilemma all too well.

She didn't think the remaining vampires and demons would act, but the dark mages… She didn't trust them. They were total rogues, and something told her Renault needed them a hell of a lot more than they needed him.

"I have a plan," she whispered back. "But we might have to spill some blood."

"Excellent." Gabriel cracked his neck and grinned at her. "Been a while since I committed mass murder. Kind of itching for it, to be honest."

"You need therapy. You know that, right?"

"Says the woman presently liquifying her former boss from the inside out? Besides, murder can be quite therapeutic, given the right circumstances."

Jaci shrugged. "Fair point. On both counts."

"Say the word, Duchanes," one of the mages called out. "I will *end* this ridiculous charade and the witch and vampire who—"

"Save it," Jaci said. With one more glance at Gabriel, she stepped forward to address the crowd. "Listen up, people. Right now, a deadly poison is coursing through Renault's bloodstream, eating him alive. The only way to save him is with an antidote located in a secure lab offsite. No one knows its location but me and my companion. So from here on out, we're in charge. Clear?"

"Duchanes," the angry mage pressed. "Give the *fucking* order."

Renault's response was little more than a shake of his head and a few broken words. "Do… do what they say."

"Bring us Cole Diamante," Gabriel demanded, "or your man dies."

Underscoring the point, he gave Duchanes a swift kick to the back, sending him sprawling face-first onto the concrete.

Jaci planted a boot on his scrawny neck, grinding down hard.

"Tick-tock," she said to the lingering goons. "The road to recovery is long and winding, and this vampire is fading fast."

"Do it," Renault croaked out, blood spilling from his lips. "Get... get the wolf."

She'd never seen the vampire so emasculated. So pathetic.

A new smile broke across her face. This time, she didn't bother hiding it.

"Jacinda Colburn." Gabriel leaned in close once more, the low timbre of his voice making her shiver. "You are absolutely *brutal*."

"Only when provoked."

"In that case, remind me not to provoke you."

"I thought you *liked* brutality, Mr. Let's Slaughter a Warehouse Full of Supernaturals For Fun."

"Not for fun, for therapy. Remember?" Gabriel shook his head and laughed, and warmth rose in Jaci's chest. Renault was nothing but a weak, docile sack of shit pinned beneath her boot. Cole would soon be back in their care. Eventually, they'd have to deal with the grays and her sister and the rest of the riffraff holing up in this warehouse, but right now, in *this* moment, it felt as if the magic of Winter Solstice had conspired with the universe to finally grant them a victory.

Jaci closed her eyes and sighed, welcoming in the return of the light, the promise of the new day awaiting them just outside the warehouse walls.

But then the mage had to go and fuck it all up.

CHAPTER FOUR

Gabriel had just enough time to grab his witch and blur her behind the farthest row of shelving before the mage unleashed hell.

A flash of blinding orange light exploded behind them, taking down a section of cages and shelving, setting loose some of the grays.

And then...

Total fucking chaos.

"Gabriel!" Jacinda gasped in his arms, trying to get her bearings after the blur.

"Time for a new plan, witch."

"The mages. You have to—"

"I'm getting you out of here." He glanced around frantically, searching for the nearest exit. Though they hadn't yet been spotted, a dozen mages and vampires stood between them and their only escape. "*Fuck.*"

"Listen to me, Prince," Jacinda said. When Gabriel met

her gaze, she sighed softly, bringing a hand up to cup his face. "You know what we have to do."

In those heart-stopping blue eyes, Gabriel read her darkest thoughts.

Fear gripped his heart, worse than what he'd felt when he'd found that vampire on top of her tonight. Worse, even, than when Duchanes had first called for her return.

"No," he said. "Absolutely not."

"We're not leaving Cole. Or Renault, for that matter. We have to fight, and our best shot is—"

"I'll come back for Cole. You need to—"

"They'll kill him the minute we walk out of here!"

"*Jacinda.* We're outnumbered, unarmed, and—"

"I told you I didn't need a weapon tonight. I *am* the weapon." She claimed his mouth in a fierce kiss, then flashed a devilish grin—the kind that would either end the world or save it.

In a dangerous whisper, she issued her command. "Detonate me, Prince."

Another explosion, grays and vampires closing in from the other end of the row, brimstone and magic sizzling in the air.

They were out of options.

"Fucking *hell*, woman." Gabriel met her gaze one last time, then shoved her behind him, shielding her from the advancing beasts. "Go."

"Gabriel—"

"Go!" he shouted over his shoulder.

She took off at a run, and Gabriel blurred into the

advancing attackers, slaughtering a pair of female vampires and pulling a huge shelving unit down on top of the grays. No use wasting time killing them—those feral ghouls wouldn't stay dead for long.

He needed to get to the mages. Now.

Back out in the open, a war erupted before Gabriel's eyes—total fucking chaos.

Grays and other half-resurrected supernaturals running rampant, vampires chasing them down, mages casting dark spells on the demons, demons attacking vampires with hell-fire. No loyalties, no clear sides, nothing but violence. Duchanes cowered in a corner, slumped against the wall and vomiting blood. From the looks of it, he'd tried to make for the exit but lost steam halfway there.

Gabriel couldn't see his woman in the chaos. Couldn't scent her. Couldn't feel her presence. He could only hope —*trust*—that she was out there somewhere. That this insane plan of hers would fucking work.

Without another thought, he plowed into the closest mage, baring his fangs and ripping out his throat. He went for the next mage, then another, and another still, dodging their magic attacks, rending hearts from bodies, severing heads. It was the cave beneath Shimmer all over again, and for those brief moments, a calm settled over Gabriel, muting everything around him but the mission. The kill. Right now, there was no Cole, no Jacinda, no tomorrow. Only the exquisite taste of blood and mayhem, the raw scent of it, the feed, the blur of carnage that didn't abate until the last mage was dead and Gabriel stood panting and wild-eyed in a pool of blood, two dozen mutilated corpses scattered at his feet.

He still clutched the bloody heart of his last victim, and as the warm slickness ran down his arm and dripped onto the floor, he finally felt it. A ripple in the air, a dark, electric thrill racing up his spine.

Jacinda.

Everything in that warehouse went still, a last collective breath before the impending annihilation.

Gabriel glanced up, caught Jacinda's gaze across the room. Dozens of demons and ghouls stood between them, the floor littered with bodies and blood, the air thick with the scents of death and rot.

But for Gabriel, there was only his witch. His demon. His entire fucking life.

Magic flared around her in bursts of silver and blue, her eyes flickering from the brightest cobalt to the darkest black. He'd slaughtered more mages tonight than he had at Shimmer, but when their dark, violent energy hit her now, she was ready for it. Didn't run from it. Didn't succumb.

She claimed it. Fucking *owned* it.

A smile touched her lips, and Gabriel dropped the mage's dead heart and nodded. *Take them down, moonflower. All of them.*

Jacinda raised her arms, muttering a spell Gabriel couldn't hear. He felt it, though; the concrete rumbled and cracked beneath his feet, the air so heavy with magic he could hardly draw breath. A hot gust of wind whipped through the warehouse, and all at once, the demons surrounding her collapsed, the black smoke of their souls floating out of their vessels, then vanishing, exorcized and obliterated.

The vampires and grays tried to mount an attack, blurring into her space, lunging and snapping, but they were no match for the ferocious witch and her arsenal of dark magic. With little more than a flick of her wrist, she turned them all to ash.

Gabriel smiled, remembering what Aiden had said the night she'd taken out the grays outside the hospital.

Jacinda Colburn *was* fucking spooky.

Certain she was out of danger, he went off in search of the wolf, leaving Jacinda to dispatch the last few pathetic monsters.

Much of the warehouse's interior now lay in smoking ruins, but the cages along the back wall remained intact, imprisoning more than a dozen shifters. Wolves, panthers, eagles, foxes, two black bears—some of them still in animal form, others in human, all of them near death. The worst though—the most gut-wrenching, harrowing sight Gabriel had ever seen—were the creatures stuck in mid-shift, caught between human and animal, moaning in abject pain.

With no way to save them—any of them—Gabriel granted them the only peace he could offer.

Instant death.

With a heavy heart, he made quick work of it, then moved on to the very end. The last three cages. He found a human corpse, likely dead for days. A young wolf who'd just taken its last breath. And there, in the last cage, tufts of dark fur poking out through the bars…

"Cole." Gabriel blew out a breath, his heart in his damn throat. Cole was emaciated and weak, his eyes rheumy, fur matted with blood both old and new, but he was alive. Fucking alive. "Bloody hell, it's good to see you, mate."

The wolf lifted his head, pressed his snout to Gabriel's palm.

"When I said we needed more intel, I didn't expect you'd go full-on method acting." Gabriel tore the cage door clean off, then reached in to stroke Cole's head, blinking the damn tears from his eyes. "You must be dying for a smoke."

The wolf yelped.

"I'll take that as a yes." As carefully as he could manage, Gabriel extracted Cole from the cage and carried him back to the main area, where Jacinda had just taken out the very last vampire.

"Cole!" she shouted, and Gabriel nodded, a wave of relief smashing right into him. His woman was alive and unharmed, the last of the magic dissipating in the air around her. His friend was severely injured, his breathing growing more erratic by the minute, but Gabriel knew he'd survive.

He fucking *had* to.

And his own heart was still beating strong—a miracle for which he'd never been more grateful.

Gabriel found a clean, unbroken patch of concrete and

gently lowered the wolf to the floor. Jacinda knelt beside them, rubbing behind Cole's ears.

"I knew you'd be here," she told him, tears streaking through the blood and grime on her face. "I knew we'd find you."

"Tell me you've still got the potion," Gabriel said.

In addition to the poison she'd whipped up for Renault, Jacinda had also made a healing potion for Cole—something to counteract the more severe effects of the silver poisoning and stabilize his condition. Isabelle and Colin would need to finish the job later, but this should at least get him through the worst of it.

Nodding, Jacinda reached into her bra to retrieve the syringe.

Gabriel lifted an eyebrow.

"What?" She shrugged, the innocence in her eyes no match for the sultriness in her voice. "You can hide all sorts of things in there."

"Hmm. Perhaps we'll play that game later."

Cole huffed out a breath and nosed Jacinda's hand.

"Hey," she said with a laugh. "I think Cole wants to play too."

"Don't get any ideas, mate." Gabriel flipped the cap off the syringe and jammed the needle into the wolf's hide, making him yelp. "Sorry. Colin got all the bedside manner in the family. I'm just the guy trying to save your life while you flirt with my woman."

Jacinda laughed again, the sound of it soothing the last

of Gabriel's worries. On this long, dark night of bloodshed and violence, that laugh felt like pure sunshine. Like hope.

"It's working," she said suddenly. "Look!"

Cole's breathing had evened out, the hazy film clearing from his eyes. He lifted his head, holding it fully upright as his limbs twitched, muscles bunching beneath the fur.

He was trying to shift.

"Don't." Gabriel placed a hand on his back. "You'll heal faster in wolf form. Besides, I'm *really* not in the mood to see your naked human arse tonight, got it?"

Cole arched his head back and let loose an ear piercing howl—closest thing to a yes Gabriel was going to get.

And the best fucking sound he'd heard all night.

Gabriel carried the wolf over his shoulders, leaving Jacinda to deal with Duchanes. The bastard was still clinging to life, though his entire body trembled, blood still leaking from his mouth.

Jacinda got him to his feet and half-carried, half-dragged him outside.

Back at the car, Gabriel got Cole situated in the backseat, then went around back to help Jacinda with their other passenger.

"All good?" he asked Jacinda.

"All good."

He popped the back hatch. "Make yourself comfortable, Duchanes."

With a swift shove from Jacinda, the vampire toppled into the trunk, too weak to fight his way out.

Blinking up at them from the cramped space, he said, "What... what do you want from me?"

"Shh," Jacinda replied, reaching for the top of the hatch. "Naptime for naughty vampires."

"No!" With an unexpected burst of new energy, Duchanes' hand shot out and grabbed her wrist, his face twisting with rage. Hunger.

But Jacinda only laughed. "I think he wants to bite me again."

"I wouldn't," Gabriel said. "Not only is she poisonous, but she'll probably kick your ass this time."

At this, he turned feral, growling and snapping, his irises red, mouth practically foaming. But try as he might, those pesky fangs just wouldn't descend.

"Yeah, that would be the poison." Jacinda yanked her wrist free and frowned at him. "Isn't it just the *worst* when you can't get it up?"

"Should've... sold you," he panted. "Slave for Kostya. He—"

Gabriel grabbed the vampire's throat and hauled him upright, bringing him nose-to-nose. Through the foul scents of blood and vomit on Duchanes' breath, Gabriel said, "You don't speak to her again. You don't touch her. You don't breathe on her. You don't even *look* at her unless and until she demands it. Is that clear?"

Duchanes laughed. Total fucking psycho.

"Let... let's settle it, Redthorne," he rasped. "Like... like men."

"You're not a man. You're a stain." Gabriel dropped his

arse back into the trunk. "Besides, you're Jacinda's prisoner. The only settling you'll be doing is with her."

"You're letting this... this *witch*... fight your battles?"

"Have you seen her fight?" Gabriel laughed. "Say what you will about the strength and speed of vampires, but from now on, my money's on her."

"Aww!" Jacinda beamed at him and wrapped a hand around his arm. "See what I mean, Ren? Isn't he just the sweetest?"

Ignoring her, Duchanes said, "Redthornes... want me dead. For decades."

"A century, actually," Gabriel said. "Because you've always been a thorn in my family's side. An annoyance at first—bit like a bad rash. Then you turned traitor. Conspirator. A would-be murderer and usurper thwarted only by his own ineptitude. So yes, perhaps all of that is cause enough to kill you, but it's certainly not your worst offense. Jacinda, on the other hand..." Gabriel leaned in close, looming over the pathetic vampire as new fury churned hot in his gut. In a low, dangerous voice, he said, "You *hurt* her, Duchanes. Repeatedly. In ways so vile I can't even bring myself to name them. Ways I'm certain will haunt her nightmares for..." Gabriel closed his eyes and clenched his jaw, fighting back a fierce wave of bile. The rage threatened to overtake him, pushing him, urging him to end this. A quick thrust of his fist, a firm grip on a feeble heart, an enemy swiftly vanquished...

A soft touch on his shoulder, a gentle breath on the air, the familiar scent of the woman he loved.

Gabriel exhaled, the rage inside him receding.

No question, Duchanes deserved to die. Right fucking now. But it wasn't Gabriel's call. Not anymore.

"So yes, Duchanes," he continued. "I *am* letting Jacinda fight this battle. Cheering her on every step of the way. And when she finally decides she's done with you, when she snaps her precious fingers and turns your rotting corpse into ash, when she turns on her heel and walks away without so much as a backward glance? That's when I'll come for you. Jacinda is going to end you. But *I'll* be the one to dump you in that nameless dirt hole, just like I promised. And do you know why?"

Duchanes shook his head, his eyes wide with new fear, his heart sputtering in the wake of his bleak new reality.

"Because Jacinda Colburn is a fucking *queen*," Gabriel said, "and handling the dust of your pathetic corpse is a task far beneath her."

At that, Gabriel slammed the hatch closed, got into the car with his woman, and drove as fast as the icy roads would allow, straight up to Ravenswood.

"Do you think Dorian will be upset?" Jacinda asked when they finally pulled into the driveway.

The manor stood sentry before them, as enigmatic and impenetrable as the vampire king himself.

A pang of unease flickered in Gabriel's gut.

He'd just survived a raid on their enemy's warehouse.

Slaughtered more mages than he cared to recall. Watched Jacinda take down a veritable army of monsters. And locked the bastard they'd been hunting for months in the trunk of his car, barely conscious.

But surviving his big brother's inevitable wrath?

Gabriel sighed. "There's a good chance I'll need to detonate you again before the day is through."

Jacinda grabbed his hand and squeezed, her laughter filling the car as readily as it filled his heart. "I'm on standby if you need me, Prince. Always."

CHAPTER FIVE

The crypts beneath Ravenswood Manor were impossibly vast—a dark, twisted labyrinth of stone passageways and alcoves so creepy Jaci wondered if Augustus Redthorne had hired his decorator straight from hell.

Definitely not the ideal place to spend your final days reflecting on your shitty life choices, but thanks to the legendary hospitality of the vampire king, that's exactly what Renault Duchanes would be doing.

Dorian *had* been upset—that much was clear from the moment he'd opened the front door and took in the filthy, bloody sight of them—but thankfully he'd stowed his anger and focused on the issue at hand, helping them get Cole to one of the bedrooms and Renault to the veritable dungeons.

Now, while the others helped Isabelle and Colin take care of the wolf, Jaci and her man were playing "Bad Cop, Worse Cop" with the bloodsucking prisoner—a last-ditch effort to suss out intel about Viansa and the bigger demonic threat.

"You missed me, Ren," she said to the bloodsucker, her smile widening. "I can tell."

Renault had just awoken from his long nap in the trunk, and now, chained to a damp wall in an even damper alcove, he trembled with rage.

Well, it was either rage, rapid onset pneumonia, the cocktail of botanical poisons cruising through his bloodstream, or all of the above—but tremble he did.

Colin had helped her turn the vampire poison into a time-release IV drip, ensuring the bastard would remain conscious and alert, but physically drained, stuck in a state of perpetual half-deadness until she was ready for him to fuck off in earnest.

Soon, she hoped. Soon as she and Isabelle finalized the binding spell. Then she'd turn him into a gray, carve out his heart, and unleash the spell on Viansa... Assuming they could find the succubus. Assuming they could keep her in one location long enough to work their magic. Assuming it actually *did* work.

Lots of assumptions there. Lots of hope. But if everything worked out, the Redthorne curse would finally be broken, Viansa's powers would be on permanent lockdown, and Jaci would be able to stake this motherfucker once and for all.

"You'll pay for this," he ground out. "You'll—"

"Listen, bloodsucker," she said. "Maybe you were

absent from class the day they taught Advanced Intimidation Tactics, but when the intimidator himself is chained up in a royal vampire dungeon and pumped full of really bad juju, his threats don't pack the same punch. Mine, however…"

She hauled off and clocked Renault in the mouth, knocking out a couple of his molars. Hurt her hand like a bitch, but *damn*—totally worth it.

Gabriel let out a soft chuckle beside her. "Brains, beauty, magic, and one hell of a right hook? I'm *definitely* keeping you."

"I'm non-returnable, Prince. You don't have a choice."

"Don't need one. Your prisoner, on the other hand… Bet he'd like to return you right about now."

In response, Renault spat out his busted teeth and a mouthful of blood. At least, Jaci assumed it was blood. Wasn't quite the right shade of red though—looked more like blackberry jam. Dark. Clumpy. Definitely the sign of a body breaking down. With the botanical poison doing its thing in his veins, the vampire's healing abilities were on permanent hiatus.

The sight made her smile all over again.

"What… what's happening to me?" he panted. His gums continued to bleed, coating his lips and tongue with the dark ooze.

"Colin Redthorne," Jaci said, shaking out her throbbing hand. "Not only does he have the hair and dimples of a Disney prince, but he's also a doctor. The two of us put our heads together, and voilà!" She fingered the line that ran from a newly installed port in his chest up to the IV bags suspended on a rack above his head. "Oh, and if you're thinking of pulling out the line, I wouldn't. Isabelle worked up a little magical insurance policy to discourage you."

"What policy?"

"Catheter." She let her gaze trail down to his crotch. "Yeah, you might not feel it now, given the level of pain you're probably in. But if you so much as sneeze and inter-rupt the flow to your veins, that little worm you call a dick will be flooded with so much poison it'll glow like a fucking lightsaber. But only for like five seconds, and then…"

Horror stretched his mouth wide. "And then?"

"It'll fall off. So, where were we?" She clapped once and nodded. "Right. Torture."

"But… wait! I—"

Jaci pressed a hand to his chest, sending a spark of hell-fire into his lungs. Flesh and blood sizzled at her command, the scent of brimstone sharp on the air.

Renault coughed and wheezed. Looking past her, he glowered at Gabriel, eyes turning red all over again. Still, the fangs stayed hidden.

"You're a traitor to your own kind, Redthorne," he snapped. "Shielding this… this *abomination*. Your father would be disgusted."

"Yes, I imagine he would be." Gabriel took a few steps closer, his voice as menacing as his gaze. "But you know something, Duchanes? It's no measure of a man's worth to garner the respect and admiration of a wretched cunt."

Renault hissed through his teeth, sending another spray of blood across his lips. "After everything he did for you. Your brothers. He made you immortal. He made you fucking vampire royalty! He made you—"

"He made us a *lot* of things, not the least of which is merciless." Gabriel wrapped a hand around Renault's throat, cutting off his air. "If you'd like to continue worshipping at the altar of Augustus Redthorne, be my guest. But if you're looking for a way to get under *my* skin, bloodsucker, best search a bit further from the family tree."

"You'll… burn in… hell," he ground out. "Both… of you."

Jaci rolled her eyes. "Been there, done that, got the T-shirt, the bumper sticker, *and* the travel mug. But Renault?" She grinned and sent another white-hot spark through his chest. "I look forward to sending *you* there real soon."

"I'd wager your ticket's already stamped," Gabriel said, fist still tight around Renault's throat. "You'll be lucky to last the rest of the day."

"Fuck… fuck you, Redthorne." He shifted his gaze to Jaci, glaring at her with a hatred that burned as hot as her hellfire. "And you… You're already… dead, *mongrel*."

Gabriel released his throat and smashed his fist into Renault's gut. "Look at her like that again, and I'll rip out your femur and use it to bash in your eye sockets."

"Excellent visual," Jaci said. "Pun intended."

Gabriel blinked at her.

"Get it?" she said, wriggling her brows. "Eye sockets? Visual?"

"You should probably stick to witchcraft and leave the comedy to the professionals."

"What? I'm hilarious! You just don't know the value of a—"

"Stop!" Renault shouted. Begged, really. "Please! I just... What the hell do you want? Why am I here? Why... why are you doing this to me?"

He coughed again, face turning red with the effort.

"Why am *I* doing this to *you*?" Jaci asked, her voice suddenly faint, as if the words had come from some other woman in some other part of the crypts. Some other realm entirely.

Gabriel took her hand. Squeezed. The momentary lightness they'd shared drained away in an instant, and Jaci sucked in a deep breath, trying to gather her strength.

For so many years, she'd fantasized about this day. A day when the man who'd tormented her for years would finally be at *her* mercy, subject to all the pains and miseries he'd unleashed on her. She'd dreamed about mutilating his body, about violating him, about burning him with hellfire from the inside out. She'd dreamed about manipulating his mind so thoroughly it would shatter, sending him into a deep, irreparable psychosis.

She'd dreamed about payback.

But now that the moment was upon her, Jaci didn't want any of those things. Those were Renault's methods. His sick pleasures. His games. Now, with the vampire chained and bound before her, completely vulnerable to her every whim, all she wanted to do was speak her fucking mind.

"For seven years, I worked for you willingly," she said. "I gave you everything you needed from a bonded witch, and a lot more you didn't need, but merely wanted. Spells for your personal gain, poisons and hexes against your so-called enemies. I performed for you, followed your orders, did whatever you needed me to do to impress your friends. You used me. Fed from me. Passed me around like a party favor. Left me to torture and torment at the hands of demons and vampires who make *you* look like a sweet little kitten."

A shudder ran through her body as the memories bombarded her—so many hands on her skin, so many mouths and tongues and teeth and fangs. Breaking, tearing, taking. Pain and threats. Power wielded and abused.

Gabriel moved closer, his hand coming to rest at the base of her neck, squeezing gently. Letting her know he was there. Giving her strength.

"I never understood why," she said. "Money? Status? Entertainment? Some sick little fantasy you could to jerk off to later?"

"No, I..." Renault coughed again. "I was only trying to—"

She held up her hand, cutting him off. "I used to lie awake at night wondering what I'd done to deserve you. Sometimes I thought it was my fault—bad karma. Other times I thought maybe I reminded you of your mother or some asshole ex-girlfriend who'd done you wrong. I kept thinking if I could just figure out what set you off so badly, I could change it. Do a little glamour spell, change my looks, my voice, something. I wanted answers, Renault. So many answers. But I needed the job—more than you'll ever understand—so I kept my mouth shut and did as I was told. All of it. Without fail. Even when it was killing me inside. Even when I knew other people—innocent people— would get hurt because of my actions. My so-called loyalty to my bonded vampire house."

A tear slid down her cheek, but she didn't brush it away. She didn't care if Renault saw her crying now. If he thought she was weak. She *wasn't* weak. She was *never* weak.

She was a fucking *survivor.*

"Now I've got you here," she continued. "Chained up. Broken. I could force you to answer my questions. To put that perpetual 'why' at rest. But you know something?" Jaci let out a laugh—quiet and breathy, but real. With every word she spoke, her heart felt stronger, brighter, as if it'd been corroded by everything she'd locked inside it and was just now remembering how to beat. To heal. "I don't give a fuck anymore, Renault. What you did was wrong, and you know it."

"But I was only—"

"No. The 'why' of it doesn't matter. Your bullshit excuses don't matter. What matters is that it's over. What matters is that you'll never hurt me—or anyone else— again."Jaci slammed her hand into his chest, hitting him with another burst of hellfire.

Through a hacking cough, he said, "So this is payback?"

"No. This is leverage." She ran her hand up the IV line again, disgust curling her lip. Confession time was over. She needed answers of a different sort—the only ones that still mattered. "You're *my* prisoner now, you sick fuck. And you're going to tell me everything I want to know about your plans."

"What… what plans?"

Jaci rolled her eyes and turned to Gabriel. "You're up, Bad Cop. Apparently, I'm still not speaking Renault's language."

"Bad cop? No, we talked about this. I'm Worse Cop. *You're* Bad Cop."

"Prove it."

"With pleasure." Gabriel grinned, then punched a hole right through Renault's thigh, wrapping his hand around the bone.

Renault howled, blood spilling from the wound, his vampire healing abilities dampened by the poison.

"You know the best thing about femurs?" Gabriel tightened his grip, unleashing another screech of pain from the prisoner. "They really are a multi-purpose bone. Good for bashing eye sockets, sure. But also excellent for cracking skulls and knocking sense into the brains of prisoners too stupid to realize they've got no other options."

"I don't know what you want!" Renault cried out. "You and Dorian… Your brothers… This witch… You took everything from me. *Everything!* Now I'm just trying to get by, and—"

"Kidnapping and torturing shifters," Gabriel said.

"Breeding grays in a warehouse in Jersey. That's you're idea of getting by?"

"I… I'm just…" Renault squeezed his eyes shut, gritting his teeth against the pain. "I'm trying to… to prepare. I need to prepare."

Gabriel finally released him, and Renault exhaled, his muscles quaking. Blood slid down his leg, pooling on the ground.

"Prepare for what, bloodsucker?" Gabriel asked.

No response.

"We know you're working for the succubus," Jaci said.

Renault's eyes widened.

"Where is she hiding out?" she continued. "Why does she need you and a bunch of dark mages to do her dirty work?"

"Succubus? I… I'm sure I don't know any succubi."

"She once called you her *favorite* vampire, Ren," Jaci said. "Now you're pretending she doesn't exist? What do you think a woman like that does to a pathetic, pencil-dicked man who denies her very existence?"

Sweat beaded across Renault's forehead, his skin growing pale from the blood loss. They didn't have much time before he passed out again.

Jaci lifted a hand and called up a ball of hellfire, letting it dance across her palm. The silver-blue flame reflected in Renault's wide, terrified eyes, and he hacked again, the fire flickering before him.

Jaci leaned in close, whispered into his ear. "We're well

past the days where you get to fuck with me, asshole. So you can either talk, or you can sizzle."

He tried to lower his head, but Jaci shoved her hand in front of his face again, letting the hellfire singe his skin.

"Fuck!" He jerked his head back and met her eyes. "The succubus... It's not her. I mean, she's not... She's just following orders."

"Viansa," Jaci said, needing the confirmation.

Renault nodded.

"Whose orders?" Jaci asked, her throat tightening. There was only one immortal being powerful enough to break Viansa. Only one whose orders the succubus had ever truly followed.

Their mother.

"Another demon," Renault said. "More powerful than... than anything. Even Viansa."

"This demon have a name?" Gabriel asked.

"Don't... don't remember."

Gabriel shoved his fingers into the hole in Renault's thigh, and Jaci braced for the inevitable confirmation. The inevitable family reunion that would end her life as well as her father's. Probably Gabriel and his brothers' lives too.

But the name that finally broke free above the tortured screams of their prisoner wasn't her mother's at all.

"Azerius!" he finally choked out. "He Whom Before All Mortals Weep. He... He Who Slaughters the Blood of—"

"Azerius?" Gabriel released Renault's femur and stepped back, his brow tight with concern. "King of Blood and Ravens?"

Renault nodded.

"Azerius," Jaci repeated, trying to remember the scraps of the stories she'd heard about the demon that'd been summoned at Bloodbath. The demon responsible for Malcolm Redthorne's death. Gabriel never talked about it, but she could've sworn… "Didn't Dorian kill him?"

"Not… completely," Gabriel said. "Dorian defeated him in battle—saved Charlotte from some kind of claim Azerius had on her soul. But according to Rogozin, Azerius can't be killed—he's just bound to hell for the next thousand years."

"He wants out," Renault said. His eyes were glassy now, his breathing sharp and erratic. "His only chance is… the hell gates. Viansa must destroy them and… harness enough power."

"Power?" Jaci asked.

Renault nodded. "So Azerius can take form. Not… not a human vessel. His *true* form."

"Here?" Jaci gasped. "But… no. Viansa can barely keep herself in this realm. How can she bring Azerius through without a vessel? Especially if he's supposed to be bound to hell for the next thousand years?"

"Fuck." Gabriel paced the alcove, leaving a trail of bloody footprints in his path. "You said you were preparing for something, Duchanes. Is this what you meant? You're helping with this… this apocalyptic resurrection? We're talking about a demon who slaughtered his entire family just because he wasn't getting enough attention from his father. A demon with the power to eradicate humanity. To eradicate *all* of us. And you, you vile piece of shit, you're preparing to *help* him?"

"Not… not preparing to help." Renault sucked in a wheezing breath, his lungs crackling. He coughed again, and his head lolled forward, blood spilling down his chest. In a final, broken whisper, he said, "Preparing for war."

CHAPTER SIX

In all their centuries of bickering, in all their petty child-hood skirmishes, in all the family drama that had done its best to wedge them apart as men and immortals both, Gabriel had never seen his eldest brother so incensed.

"*Explain,*" Dorian demanded, his jaw clenched so tight Gabriel thought his teeth might shatter.

The two of them were locked away in the study, alone for the first time since Gabriel and Jacinda had shown up on Dorian's doorstep hours earlier with a broken wolf, an unconscious vampire, and little time for conversation. A roaring fire cast the room in a soft, warm glow, but the mood was anything but cozy.

Gabriel headed straight for the bar, helping himself to a glass of bourbon. Dorian was already three drinks in, but he poured his brother another scotch anyway, hoping it might help the story go down better.

"We got the call in the middle of the night," he said, passing Dorian the glass. "Duchanes had taken Cole. Said he'd trade him for Jacinda."

"You knew it was a trap."

Gabriel nodded.

"Yet you marched right in anyway, guns blazing."

"Not guns so much as magic, but—"

"For fuck's sake, Gabriel. Do you have any idea what could've happened? A vampire and a witch, taking on a warehouse full of grays, dark mages, enemy vampires, demons—"

"What choice did I have? He was going to kill Cole, Dorian. Cole!"

Dorian cursed under his breath. Tossed back half his drink in one go. "You should've called me. As much as you excel at violence, going in there alone to commit a mass murder—"

"It was the only way to pull this off. If Duchanes had caught so much as a *whiff* of an attack plan, Cole would've been dead in a heartbeat, and Jacinda and I would've swiftly followed."

"So you decided—without a consult from me, mind you —vigilante mode was the better bet?"

"Jacinda had a plan. A damned good one at—"

"You're saying this was her idea?" Dorian shook his head, a bitter laugh escaping. "I don't buy it. This has your brand of recklessness and disregard stamped *all* over it, little brother."

Little brother.

Gabriel seethed. As if Dorian would ever let him forget.

"What would you have done, Dorian? Leave your friend to torture and death? No way. No fucking way."

"*I* would've called my family. Called our allies and made a plan that—"

"There was no time. Besides, Rogozin would've given this mission a hard pass. He's got no interest in risking his hellspawn arse for a lone wolf. "

"He's our ally. Why can't you accept that?"

"Rogozin can't be trusted. He's a bloody demon, Dorian. A demon!"

Anger flared in Dorian's eyes. "So is the woman with whom you share your bed. Perhaps you'll bear that in mind the next time you decide—"

"How can you even *make* that comparison? Alexei Rogozin is the head of a demonic crime syndicate. A hellspawn thug who trafficks human souls and damns innocent people to hell. Jacinda saved Charlotte's life—she nearly died because of it."

Dorian's hand tightened on his glass, the color draining from his face. "I don't need the reminder."

"Apparently you do." Gabriel turned away from him, unable to bear the weight of his brother's judgmental gaze. His scorn.

Why the fuck had he even come here?

Why had he thought, for one stupid moment, that Dorian would understand? Would offer anything but criticism and rebuke?

"This was a bad idea," Gabriel said. "Sorry to have

disturbed you, *highness.*" He set down his glass and had just taken a step toward the door when he felt Dorian's hand on his shoulder—a brief squeeze that stopped him in his tracks.

"Gabriel, wait. Please. I…" Dorian sighed, stirring the air behind Gabriel's neck. "You know I care for Jacinda. This has nothing to do with her origins and everything to do with… Well, you're in love with her. You, of all vampires, fell in love with a demon."

"Do you have a point, brother? If so, I suggest you get to it."

"If you can trust Jacinda, why can't you at least consider the possibility that Rogozin is on our side as well?"

"Simple probability. Half the monsters in Duchanes' house of horrors were demons—Chernikov's leftovers, Rogozin's, unaligned—doesn't matter. They're all working with Duchanes and Viansa to destroy the hell gates and take over this realm."

"We've known that for some time. It doesn't explain why you stormed in there alone to slaughter an army. Why there's an injured wolf upstairs and a piece-of-shit vampire rotting in my crypts. Why you—"

"Should I have left Duchanes in Jersey?" Gabriel finally turned to face him, frustration thickening the air between them again, as stuffy and familiar as Ravenswood itself. "Dropped him off at the bus station perhaps? Bought him a ticket to Miami and sent him on his merry way?"

"For fuck's sake, Gabriel. I'm not upset you brought him here. Given the options, it was certainly the best choice."

"Then what the fuck is your problem, highness? Cole is safe. We took out Duchanes' entire Newark operation—everyone present at the warehouse, anyway. We bought ourselves more time for Jacinda and Isabelle to figure out this binding spell. And most importantly, we captured our primary enemy—something *you've* been failing at for decades. Jacinda and I outsmarted him in one night, and you've got the balls to say—"

"Outsmarted him. Yes, you've always been the clever one, haven't you?"

"And you've always been the controlling one, though I see you're pulling double duty now, making up for the loss of our resident smug bastard. Surely Malcolm would be pleased to know you've taken up the mantle of—"

"*Don't*," Dorian warned. "Don't you even say his name."

"Is that an order from the king? Or just the weak defense of a guilty conscience?"

It was the wrong thing to say—the most *abominable* thing—and Dorian gasped and staggered backward as if the words had physically shoved him.

Wounded him.

Fuck.

Gabriel hadn't meant to bring up their dead brother—not like that. He'd just grabbed for the closest, sharpest weapon in his head and hurled it forth, consequences be damned.

And now...

"Dorian, I... That isn't... I didn't..."

The words died on his lips. It was far too late for backpedaling now.

With no more warning but a flash of fury in his eyes, Dorian blurred into him and shoved him against the wall, forearm pressed to his throat, his entire body trembling with the force of his pain. His rage.

For the briefest instant, Gabriel saw the old Dorian in his eyes—the one the press had named the Crimson City Devil. The one Gabriel had fled from fifty years ago. The one consumed by violence and bloodlust, all traces of humanity gone.

But then Dorian blinked, and suddenly those deep brown eyes held nothing but anguish. Nothing but the same grief that threatened to choke Gabriel as readily as Dorian's powerful grip.

Their arguments were forgotten.

In that moment, they were no longer vampires. No longer adversaries. No longer the cruel, vicious monsters their father had molded in his image.

In that moment, Gabriel and Dorian Redthorne were just two brothers swimming against the treacherous currents of loss and death, wondering if they'd ever find their way back to shore.

Wondering if the shore even existed anymore.

With a defeated sigh, Dorian finally released him.

When he spoke again, his voice was soft and broken. Exhausted—and not just from the curse wreaking havoc on their blood.

"Congratulations, brother. You managed to go… what? Two months without throwing Mac's death in my face?" Dorian turned away and reached for the bottle of scotch. The medicine. "Epic restraint. Truly commendable."

"Dorian, I don't blame you. It wasn't—"

"Just go, Gabriel." He took a swig from the bottle, then nodded toward the door. "You know the way out by now. You've certainly taken it enough times before today."

Indignation. Rejection. A deep, dark sadness.

All of it sliced through Gabriel's heart at once, ripping apart the seams he'd been trying so desperately since his return to New York—since his return to Dorian—to mend.

Gabriel stared at his brother. At the amber firelight reflecting in his eyes. In the bottle.

For a brief instant, he wanted nothing more than to do just as Dorian had asked—turn his back. Walk out. Make his last grand escape from all the pain and strife and regret this family—this entire fucking *life*—had brought him.

He closed his eyes. Took a deep, ragged breath. Counted the cracks and pops of the firewood, the defeated beats of his own broken heart.

Opening his eyes, he glanced up at Dorian one last time. But rather than the brother who'd loomed large in every one of his memories, now he saw only the girl.

She stood beside the fireplace, dress blackened with old blood. Her face was full and pale once more, but her eyes were still the same dark pits he'd seen at the cabin, fresh blood streaking down her cheeks. The skin had torn away from her hands and feet, exposing the rotting gray bones beneath.

She lifted her hand, pointed a mangled finger at the door. Smiled her grim, twisted smile.

Leave him, Prince, her dark whisper echoed through his head. *It's what you do. It's what you* always *do…*

Gabriel turned toward the door, but couldn't bring himself to take another step. His muscles twitched, his legs aching from the effort of holding back, his head full of whispers and ghosts, everything inside him burning for the freedom that existed on the other side of that door.

Dying for it.

But still, he couldn't leave.

In the quiet darkness of his own mind, his own broken heart, he recalled the silent vow he'd made the day Colin had reported on Zachary Colburn.

Never again.

Never again would he abandon his family, no matter how bad things got.

No matter how deeply his brothers made him ache.

He turned back toward the fireplace. The ghost girl was gone. Dorian stared into the flames, the bottle of scotch dangling loosely between two fingers.

Gabriel took another breath. Tried to brace himself for whatever Dorian would throw at him next. An insult? The bottle? Another blur against the wall, finally tearing out his throat?

But the anger seemed to be receding, and when Dorian

finally spoke again, his voice was soft and vulnerable, as broken as Gabriel felt on the inside.

"After you left New York, I spent the next fifty years convincing myself I was better off without you. *All* of you." Dorian ran his hand along the mantle, his head bowed toward the flames. "Colin with his obsessive thirst for knowledge, so much like our father it bloody terrifies me. You and your reckless scheming. Your temper. The way you look at me as if I'm supposed to have all the answers. Malcolm and his superiority complex. That smug, Malcolm-knows-best way he always…" Dorian closed his eyes and brought the bottle to his lips. Took a deep drink. "But then Father died, and all of you just… You returned to me."

Gabriel reached for his bourbon again, not sure what to say. He'd spent the last fifty years doing much the same, telling himself he didn't need his family. His brothers. Trying like hell to bury his memories of them under a pile of drugs and booze and blood and death.

"Getting you back," Dorian said softly, "getting my *family* back…" He shook his head, then finally turned to meet Gabriel's eyes again, his own glazed with emotion. "It's a cruel thing to be given a gift you didn't even realize you'd wanted—*needed*—only to have it taken from you the moment you've finally come to accept it. Losing another brother… I can't go through it again, Gabriel. I *won't*."

You won't, Gabriel wanted to say. But how could he know that? How could he make that promise? All of them were living on borrowed time. Immortality didn't protect them from that.

In fact, being vampires only seemed to bring death that much closer.

"Gabriel, you need to know…" Dorian returned his gaze to the fire, his words weighted with guilt and shame. "Malcolm's death was… I never meant for… He didn't even…"

His voice broke, shoulders tight from the effort of holding back whatever darkness, whatever despair threatened to break free.

Gabriel approached him slowly. Put a hand on his shoulder—the only show of affection he dared. "It wasn't your fault. Mac just—"

"Don't," Dorian whispered, but this time it wasn't an order. Just a sad, desperate plea that punched a fresh hole through Gabriel's heart. "Please, Gabriel. I… I can't. I just can't."

Gabriel felt Malcolm all around him then, a sudden overwhelming presence rising like smoke, filling the room, filling his lungs, filling his every cell. Malcolm's voice—that stiff, self-satisfied tone. The scent of him—expensive cologne hiding the hint of bergamot beneath. His laugh—the real one, the rarest one.

And there, right before he faded again, came Gabriel's last memory of the man, standing inside Bloodbath among the carnage, his fist deep inside Charlotte's chest, one breath from tearing out her heart.

Dorian and Gabriel sat in the chairs before the fire and finished their drinks in silence, each lost in his own memories, his own unanswered questions.

His own guilt.

When Gabriel finally drained the last of his bourbon, he looked at Dorian, let out a heavy sigh, and said, "I need to tell you what Duchanes said about Viansa. About who's *really* calling the shots on this demon plot."

CHAPTER SEVEN

"Azerius."

The name echoed through the study like a phantom, the first word Dorian had spoken in the long moments since Gabriel had given his full report.

"We're not sure if Duchanes is helping him or trying to mount a defense for his inevitable arrival," Gabriel said now, "but either way, I saw the look in his eyes when admitted who was pulling the strings. I believed him, Dorian. Azerius wants out, and apparently, he's got Viansa doing his dirty work. If he succeeds…"

Gabriel didn't need to spell it out.

"How is this even possible?" Dorian asked.

"I'm not sure the 'how' matters so much as the 'what the fuck are we going to do about it.'"

"We need to bring Rogozin in on this. Azerius is the patron saint of his organization. Well, whatever the demonic version of a patron saint is."

"Patron saint. Right." Gabriel laughed. "So when it comes time to pick sides, you think Rogozin will remain loyal to the vampire king over his demonic overlord? Fuck, Dorian. Every demon in his organization is tattooed with the white raven."

Back before the Redthornes and the Rogozin crew were so-called allies, Gabriel had tortured enough of the Russian demons to see it—the white raven branding their skin, honoring the King of Blood and Ravens himself.

"My understanding is Rogozin doesn't have any love for the demon Azerius," Dorian said. "It's more of a fear-based relationship. A historical obligation, if you will."

"Hmm. Where have I seen this show before?" Gabriel rolled his eyes, but at this point, he wasn't even mad anymore. The whole thing was getting downright comical. "Oh, that's right! Our own dysfunctional family."

"Yes, the dynamic does have a tinge of the familiar, doesn't it?"

"Father's laughing at us. You know that, right?"

"Father was incapable of laughter in life. I suspect an eternity in hell isn't doing much for his sense of humor."

Gabriel tapped his empty glass on the table beside him, trying to figure out what came next. "Okay, highness. Let's say your man Rogozin *can* be trusted. Let's say he's bloody well in *love* with you, his loyalty unwavering, tattoos be damned. Even with all that, what could he actually *do* for us?"

"Honestly, I have no idea. Not specifically."

"Then what's the point?"

Dorian sighed. "I'm the vampire king, Gabriel. I can't claim to want peace in the supernatural community if I'm not even willing to trust my own allies—to ask for unity and support in the face of a greater threat."

"I understand that. I'm just not convinced Rogozin isn't *part* of that threat. I don't trust him, Dorian. I'm sorry, but I just don't."

"I'm not asking you to trust Rogozin. I'm asking you to trust *me*."

Gabriel closed his eyes. There were a thousand things running through his head—his doubts about Rogozin, his fears about Azerius taking revenge on Dorian, his unanswered questions about Malcolm's death, his worries for Jacinda, disgust at his own failings and weaknesses in the face of an impending war that could wipe humans and supernaturals off the map…

But in the end, all he could do was nod.

It was a new thing for both of them, this trusting business. But like Dorian had said about wanting peace, how could Gabriel claim he wanted reconciliation with his family if he wasn't even willing to meet Dorian halfway?

Besides, no matter how brutally they fought, no matter what terrible things he said in the heat of the moment, the truth was, Gabriel *did* trust his oldest brother. More than Dorian realized.

"Can we meet with him?" Gabriel finally asked. "Together, I mean? I can fill him in about what we've learned and see if he's got any more insight on Azerius and the greater demonic plot."

"You're willing to take the risk?" Dorian's eyebrows lifted in surprise. "To share what we know about Azerius?"

"If you think it's the right call, I'm backing you, brother."

A tiny smile curved Dorian's mouth, and he nodded. "I'll make the arrangements tomorrow."

"Good." Gabriel rose from the chair, a wave of exhaustion washing over him. He missed his woman. Needed her in his arms. Needed to sink deep inside her and know, after all the bloodshed, after all the risks she'd taken tonight, she was truly okay. "If there's nothing else, I'm heading upstairs."

"Off to bed, then? But you haven't murdered anyone in hours. How *ever* will you sleep with such a light conscience?" Dorian grinned and made a show of pulling out his cell. "Perhaps I'll phone Rogozin now, see if he might be willing to sacrifice a few underlings for the cause."

Gabriel laughed. "So his royal highness tells jokes now? Shall I issue a press release? Do you need a stage manager or an agent or—"

"What I need, little brother, is to know that *you're* sleeping soundly under my roof, that *Cole* is back to his smart-ass, pot-smoking self, and that *Duchanes* is well on his way to becoming the world's first immortal heart donor. Can you guarantee me all of that?"

"Two out of three. Unfortunately, I won't be getting sleep tonight. Not for a good long while, anyway." Gabriel took the bottle of scotch from Dorian's hand and downed the last of it. "I've got a witch to punish. One with an annoying penchant for recklessness and disregard, among other things."

"A match made in hell." Dorian laughed. "Do try to keep the damage to my guest room at a minimum."

Gabriel smirked, his cock already throbbing as he thought of all the wicked things he wanted—*needed*—to do to her. "No promises, highness. No fucking promises."

CHAPTER EIGHT

The manor was mostly silent when Gabriel finally headed upstairs, save for the rhythmic snoring of the wolf behind one of the bedroom doors. It sounded human. It sounded normal.

Gabriel pressed his hand to the door and closed his eyes, wiping the memory of Cole's emaciated wolf form from his mind. Cole was a tough, take-no-prisoners bastard, and he'd come through the worst of it. He was going to be just fine.

"Welcome back, mate," he whispered.

In the guest suite at the end of the hall, Gabriel finally found his witch, freshly showered and stretched out on the bed in a T-shirt.

Only a T-shirt, the thin fabric clinging to her damp curves, the dark shadows of her nipples making his mouth water for the taste of her. His gaze trailed down to her thighs, strong and muscular, smooth, lickable.

Biteable.

Gabriel closed his eyes, fighting back a shiver at the rush of memories. Those thighs parting for him beneath the rose bushes, his fangs piercing the silky flesh, the warm smoke of her blood filling his mouth…

"Everything okay, Prince? You look a little…"

"Thirsty," he whispered, opening his eyes and blinking away the memories.

Jacinda sat at the edge of the bed now, the T-shirt bunched up around her waist. She shifted her legs, and Gabriel caught a glimpse of bare flesh, no panties, nothing in the way of his impending kiss.

With a teasing smirk on her smart little mouth, she asked, "Should I get you some water?"

He watched her for a long moment, gaze roving the dips and curves of her body, the shape of her face, the curls of damp, moonlight-colored hair just starting to frizz.

Something grabbed him then. Reached right into his chest and squeezed. The force of it nearly buckled his knees.

"You nearly died tonight, Jacinda," he said softly. Darkly. "More than once. All because you—"

"*Nearly* isn't *actually*, though. Right?" She hopped up from the bed and slid her hands over his shoulders, flashing the devastating smile that never failed to disarm him. "That's the bright side."

Gabriel trailed his hands down her back, sliding over the bare, soft curves of her arse, lifting her easily.

She wrapped her thighs around his hips, and he

captured her mouth in a kiss, holding her close, needing to feel her heartbeat, needing to know she was truly okay. Alive. Safe.

His.

"The bright side, little moonflower," he said when they finally broke for air, "is that we've got nowhere to be for a good eight or ten hours. Which gives me plenty of time to mete out your… punishment."

He stole another kiss, then set her back on her feet. Slowly, he removed his clothing, letting her enjoy the show.

"You're punishing me, huh?" she teased.

"Lose that shirt."

"Why?"

"Because it's in my way."

"No, I mean…" She tugged the shirt over her head and tossed it onto the bed, her eyes sparkling. "Why am I being punished?"

"For flirting."

"You can't be serious." Jacinda laughed. "With who? The panther guy?"

"No, Jacinda. Not the panther guy." He stepped toward her again and palmed her breasts, her nipples warm and hard against his skin. "With death."

She looped her arms around his neck and gave him that naughty little smirk, but this time, Gabriel wasn't swayed. She really *had* flirted with death tonight. He'd walked in on it, seen it unfold in an instant. That first vampire who'd taken her down… He had every intention of destroying her.

Devil's balls, if Gabriel had shown up five seconds later,

Jacinda would've been eviscerated, and he would be several hours into a bloody rampage that would make the Crimson City Devil look like a fucking mosquito.

The memory of that vampire scraped him raw on the inside, and he dug his fingers into her hips, overcome with the sudden need to mark her. To claim her as if that alone would keep her safe.

"You will *never* come so close to death again," he said. Then, in a low growl, "Now get on your knees and—"

"Pray?" She pressed her palms together and shot him a smile full of feigned innocence, slowly dropping to her knees.

Gabriel fisted his cock, already hard and ready. "Worship if you must, but prayers won't save you tonight."

"You sure about that?"

"I've got this problem, see."

"A huge one, from the looks of it." She let her eyes roam over his cock, her heart rate kicking up, the scent of her desire filling his senses. "Also, not a problem. Not a punishment, either. Not in my expert opinion."

"Clearly not." He took another step closer. Stroked himself. Took great pleasure in the soft hitch of her breath, the darkening of her cheeks as her blood rushed to the surface. "The problem, little moonflower, is... Well, it's more of a paradox, actually. Watching you vanquish our enemies terrified me to the core. But it also made me *rock* fucking hard for you, and I'm just not sure how to reconcile the two."

"Hmm. Quite the conundrum."

"You have *no* idea."

Fire flashed in her eyes, a shock of magic and heat that made his balls ache.

He guided the tip of his cock to her mouth, gently tracing the outline of her lips.

"Open your mouth for me, moonflower," he said, the softness in his voice belying his dark, raging lust.

She parted those lush lips for him, taking him in with a soft hum that buzzed across his sensitive flesh.

"Deeper," he murmured, sliding his hands into her hair. "All the way in. Just like… Fucking *hell*, woman. Just like that."

Jacinda let out another soft moan and reached for the base of his cock, her tongue working him hot and fast, every delicious stroke making him shiver. The way she touched him, the way she licked and teased, the scent of her, the still-damp hair tangled around his fingers, the light in her eyes when she gazed up at him…

No one—nothing—had ever made Gabriel feel so alive. So on *fire* with need and wanting and a deep, infinite love that threatened to consume.

That's where his feelings for her lived, thrived, somewhere in that space between devotion and obsession, between passion and madness. Half the time he didn't know which side of the line he walked—only that a single one of her kisses lit a raging inferno inside his once-frozen heart, and every time she whispered his name, he wanted to carve open his chest and burn down the world for her.

Jacinda dragged her lips back along his cock, then took

him in deep once more, licking, sucking, her mouth hot and velvet-soft and damn near perfect.

But like she'd said earlier, *nearly* wasn't *actually*, and right now, Gabriel needed the real deal. The *actual* perfect he could only find in the silky, seductive haven between her thighs.

He pulled back with every intention of dropping to the floor, pushing her onto her back, and claiming her with a deep, punishing thrust she'd feel for the rest of eternity.

But Jacinda wasn't giving in so easily. With a mischievous sparkle in her eyes, she fisted him tight once more, bringing her mouth right back to his cock, her tongue darting out to dance across the tip as she stroked him faster and harder and…

Bloody hell…

Five more seconds and he was past the point of no return, no more able to pull out of her mouth than he could walk out of her life.

"Right there, Jace. *Right* fucking there. That's… oh, fuck. *Fuck*…" Gabriel sucked in a breath and held it, heart slamming against his ribs as the heat exploded in his chest and crept down his spine, lower, lower still, finally gripping his balls and pushing him past the fucking brink. He came hot and hard, a surge of pleasure sweeping through him with such ferocity it made the room spin.

Everything in his body pulsed and shivered, heart still pounding, the room a blur of colors and shapes. It felt like forever before he could see again, before he could form words, before he could look down at the beautiful, naked woman on her knees before him and thank the fucking devil for witches and demons both.

For *this* witch and demon.

Gabriel pulled out of Jacinda's mouth, and she looked up at him and grinned, her eyes dancing with mischief. "Did I solve your problem, Prince?"

"Hmm. I'm afraid *you're* the one with the problem now, moonflower." He scooped her into his arms, then threw her down on the bed and climbed on top of her, claiming her mouth in a bruising kiss.

In minutes he was hard for her again.

Jacinda shifted beneath him, and he slid between her thighs, whispering her name as he sank deep inside, finally finding the pure, absolute perfection he'd been missing.

A soft sigh of pleasure drifted from her lips, and she looked up at him and smiled, her eyes dark with desire. "Still not seeing the problem here, Prince."

"Oh, I'm just getting started."

Jacinda laughed, a sound that called forth a fierce wave of protectiveness. There was nothing he wouldn't do to keep that smile on her face forever.

He slowed his thrusts, then stopped, reaching up to brush the hair from her eyes. "I'm proud of you, Jace."

Another smile. Another sparkle glittering in her eyes. "Yeah?"

"The way you handled yourself at the warehouse. That shit with Duchanes... All of it. You're a fucking... hell, I don't even have the word for it."

"Badass. The word you want is badass."

Gabriel laughed, tracing the outline of her mouth with his thumb. "*Now* who's developing the hero complex?"

"Not that I'm trying to steal your thunder or anything, Prince." Jacinda grinned at him again, but then her smile faded, her eyes turning serious. "Thanks for having my back last night. I keep playing over the raid in my mind... Things could've gone very differently if you hadn't—"

"Don't say it," he whispered urgently. "Don't even think it." He kissed her again, if only to stop her from giving voice to his fears. "I promise you, Jacinda. There will never be a time when I *don't* have your back."

She brushed her fingertips along his jaw and nodded, and he rolled his hips and slid in deeper, harder, Jacinda's breathy moans calling once more to his own fierce, carnal desire. It wasn't long before she was close to losing control, her body tightening around him, the familiar quake in her thighs spreading down her legs, a sheen of sweat glistening on her chest.

"Gabriel," she breathed.

"I know, little moonflower. I know."

She reached up to touch his face again, her eyes glazing with emotion, mouth parted, thighs clenched tight, seconds from shattering...

"I've never felt anything like this," she whispered.

"Nor have I."

"Tell me it's real."

"You don't need the words, love. You just need to feel it." He grabbed her hand, pressed it to his chest. Beneath her touch, his heart beat strong and steady. "Trust this. Trust us."

"I do. I… I'm… Gabriel…" Her eyelids fluttered closed, and Gabriel shifted between her thighs, brushing over her clit as he plunged inside her once more.

Jacinda gasped, arching her back to take him in deeper, clutching his arms as the orgasm finally took hold. It rocked through her entire body, making her writhe, making her beg, making her lose control.

"Look at me." Gabriel fisted her hair, forcing her to open her eyes as she rode out the intense, white-hot pleasure. "You *belong* to me, Jacinda Colburn. Understand?"

It wasn't a threat, wasn't a bedroom game, wasn't about her body or all the ways he loved to make her come.

No, the sort of belonging Gabriel was talking about now was a promise. A vow he was making, once and for all, to protect her. To cherish her. To *truly* love her in a way no one else ever had—a way Gabriel himself had never thought possible. Not until he'd taken her prisoner and she'd glared at him across the bar, folded her arms across her chest, and promised to grind his bones into dust.

Breathless beneath him, Jacinda nodded and smiled and whispered his name, and that was all it took.

Gabriel came in another dizzying, blinding-hot rush, burying his face in the crook of her neck, inhaling her scent, tasting her skin, committing her to his every fucking cell as the breath left his lungs and his body quivered and his heart burst a thousand times over and then—at her lightest touch, her softest laugh—stitched itself back together, again and again and again.

After a long, languid moment, Gabriel finally pulled back to look at her once more, and in the dawn of her smile, Gabriel found his home.

"Partners," she said softly. "Always."

She lifted her head and brushed the sweetest kiss to his mouth, then wriggled out from beneath him, reaching for her pillow on the other side of the bed.

"Weary of your punishments already?" he teased.

"I kind of love how your idea of punishing me is giving me the most epic orgasm of the century." She adjusted the pillow beneath her head and sighed. "Aren't you tired?"

"Exhausted." Gabriel laughed. "And you?"

"Just trying to figure out what's so damn funny all of a sudden."

He rolled back on top of her and lowered his mouth to her earlobe, capturing it between his teeth. With a soft growl, he said, "What's funny, little moonflower, is that you think one epic orgasm of the century means I'm anywhere *near* finished with you."

CHAPTER NINE

By the time the late-morning sun roused Gabriel from a dark and dreamless sleep, Jacinda and the rest of his family were already gathered in the Ravenswood kitchen, the remnants of a monstrous pancakes-and-bacon breakfast scattered across the table, all of them laughing at something Cole had just said.

A welcome sight.

"The stoner wolf returns to the land of the living," Gabriel said. He'd meant it as a joke, but his voice broke at the end, an unexpected surge of emotion tightening his throat.

"Good as new and twice as handsome." Cole raked a hand through his scraggly hair, revealing an angry red scar on the left side of his forehead, slicing down through the eyebrow. "Jacinda tells me the ladies love a man with sexy battle scars. It's a good thing, too, 'cause I got about a dozen more in places that ain't suitable to show at the breakfast table. But if you ask me *real* nice—"

"Total health code violation," Charlotte said. Then, to Gabriel, "Be grateful you slept in. Took Dorian half the morning to wrestle him into his pants."

"A traumatic experience I'm still trying to scrub from my memory," Dorian said.

Cole laughed. "You two never let me have any fun."

Gabriel nodded, but couldn't bring himself to share in their laughter. It was his damn fault the wolf had been captured. Tortured. Carved up like a fucking pot roast. If not for Jacinda's quick thinking and absolute disregard for her own safety, the wolf would probably be dead.

"You and little miss hot-pants over here saved my ass," Cole said, winking at Jacinda across the table. When he looked up at Gabriel again, his face was stern and serious. "So whatever bullshit story's runnin' through your skull, Little Red, let it go."

The wolf held Gabriel's gaze for a beat, making him hot and uncomfortable. Didn't matter what Cole said. Logic wasn't a remedy for guilt—not in the hundreds of years Gabriel had been trying to make it so, and certainly not today.

Still, he smiled and smacked Cole on the back, then took a seat next to Jacinda and grabbed her fork, spearing a blueberry pancake she'd abandoned on her plate.

"Cole's right, Gabriel," Isabelle said over the rim of her teacup. "You and Jacinda saved his life."

"Seems to me you and Colin had a role in that as well,"

Gabriel said. "Cole was a hell of a lot uglier when we brought him in yesterday. Well, uglier than usual."

"Cole's condition has improved tenfold," she said. "He's getting stronger by the hour."

"Damn straight I am." Cole curled his hand around the side of his mouth, pretending to whisper. "If only Nurse Ratchet here'd serve me my breakfast of choice, my condition would be perfect."

"Whiskey and cigarettes aren't breakfast," the witch said. "Especially for a wolf who spent the last few days getting pumped full of silver."

"Yeah, zero stars on that one," Cole said with another laugh. "Do *not* recommend."

Gabriel glanced around the room, noticing a few faces missing from the group. Colin's absence wasn't unusual—on the occasions he visited Ravenswood, he spent most of his time down in the crypts in their father's old laboratory. But Aiden and Sasha had become a somewhat permanent fixture around the breakfast nook, especially now that Charlotte was living here.

"Vampire Ken and Underage Barbie aren't joining us this morning?" he asked.

"Sasha just got back from a ski trip with her roommate," Charlotte said. "She'll be here tomorrow morning, weather permitting. Aiden's keeping Colin company in the crypts. They're monitoring Duchanes and reading through some of your father's journals."

"Dear Diary," Gabriel mocked, shoveling in another mouthful of pancake. "Today I frightened off some children at the park, stole an old woman's diabetes medication, and bit off the head of a live barn owl. Sadly, I still haven't received my #1 Supervillain medallion from the Association of Deplorable Twats."

Dorian rose from the table and headed for the fridge, retrieving two bottles of blood. Passing one to Gabriel, he said, "They're looking for more intel on Azerius."

Azerius. The very name sent a shudder down Gabriel's spine.

They'd first learned about the demon a couple of months ago when Charlotte discovered an ancient dagger hidden in one of Dorian's sculptures. An expert in art and antiquities, she'd thought it was Russian in origin, but after piecing together some of the demonic lore from Isabelle and the cryptic notes Augustus had left behind, they learned the truth. The dagger was actually a hell-forged weapon crafted by a demon called Azerius—a demon whom Augustus had called upon centuries earlier for help usurping the throne from House Kendrick.

What they knew about Azerius was limited—according to legend, he was the son of a disgraced god and eventually slaughtered his sixteen siblings and their entire families in a bid to reclaim his father's elusive attention. When that failed, Azerius made a dark bargain with the old gods of his father's time, ultimately rising in power as a demon who sews chaos on human battlefields and unleashes an unquenchable thirst for violence and brutality.

Some demonic factions—including Rogozin's organization—venerated him as a god.

And he *definitely* had a hard-on for Dorian—more than likely, removing the vampire king's head from his body was at the very top of Azerius' things-to-do-when-you're-topside bucket list.

"So who's the greater threat right now?" Gabriel asked. "Azerius? Viansa?"

"Don't forget the Keepers of the Dark Flame," Isabelle said.

"We took out a bunch of them at the warehouse," Gabriel said.

"A bunch, but not all." Isabelle set down her teacup. "I infiltrated a Solstice gathering in Brooklyn. It was outdoors—I wasn't spotted."

"What did you learn?" he asked.

"I'm afraid the cult is much larger—and much more organized—than we feared. They never mentioned Viansa or Azerius by name at the gathering, but it's clear they're working to bring the demons to power. They've got various factions across the metro area, all of them preparing spells and rituals designed to forge a direct connection to hell—the kind of magic even the darkest of dark witches know better than to experiment with."

"Colin's been hearing whispers at the hospital about ritual murders," Dorian said. "The police haven't given an official statement, but he's seen some of the bodies and is confident it's the Dark Flame mages."

"How can he tell?" Gabriel asked.

"The burns and carvings on their torsos are consistent

with the red sigil you and Jacinda described seeing in the cave at Shimmer."

"*Viansa's* sigil," Jacinda said, as if Gabriel needed the reminder.

His insides burned at the memory of that night. The fucking mages who nearly sacrificed Jacinda. He reached under the table for her hand, holding it tight against his thigh.

"Viansa's been topside for weeks," Jacinda said. "She needs sexual energy to survive and death energy to stay. We knew the bodies would start turning up eventually."

"Unfortunately," Isabelle said, "there are likely even more of them yet to be discovered. And if we don't stop this thing she's plotting with Azerius…"

She didn't need to elaborate.

"We still need to figure out a binding spell for Viansa," Jacinda said, seemingly undaunted by the immensity of the task. "If we can trap her here without her power, we can force her to talk. Not just about my father's soul, but about Azerius and his plans."

"And without the succubus and her loyal mages working magic on Azerius' behalf," Isabelle said, "there's a chance the demon can't manifest here at all—true form or otherwise."

Cole poured a shot of whiskey into his coffee and stirred, ignoring Isabelle's sharp glare. "Far as you know, any demon ever manifest here in his true form?"

"No. And if they did, we'd all be in some *serious* shit."

"Define serious," Gabriel said.

"According to the legends, any human who looks upon the true face of a demon will succumb instantly to a madness so severe, he'll set himself on fire just to burn the memory from his mind."

Gabriel downed the last of his blood, then stared out the windows behind the breakfast nook, squinting into the morning light. Outside, a thick blanket of snow covered the grounds of Ravenswood, glittering and pristine. A cardinal landed on a bare tree branch just beyond the pane, a bright slash of color against the snow.

How was it possible they could be sitting here on this breathtakingly perfect winter morning, enjoying pancakes and one another's company when somewhere in the same universe, a legion of demons plotted to eradicate their very existence?

Everyone's very existence?

Nine million humans in the metro area alone, and now Gabriel pictured them all lining up in the streets, dousing themselves in gasoline and setting themselves ablaze just to escape the horrors of one demon. One fucking monster.

And that was just here in New York. If Azerius manifested in his true form outside of hell, how long until the entire human population was nothing but ash in the wind?

"Self-immolation?" Dorian asked. "That's… that's just insanity, Isabelle. Utter insanity."

"Hell's most fearsome demons are not known for their sanity," she replied.

Cole dropped the spoon into his mug with a clatter. "You know, one day I'm gonna show up here for a nice family breakfast, and you Redthornes are gonna be talkin' about—oh, I don't know. Regular family bullshit. The kind that don't end with a demon setting the world on fire or a vampire chained up in a dungeon."

"Not likely, mate." Aiden appeared in the kitchen entryway, his face as pale and gray as the layer of ash covering his clothes. "Hate to be the bearer of more irregular, non-family bullshit, but Renault Duchanes is dead."

CHAPTER TEN

Ash and brimstone hung heavy in the air, stinging the back of Jaci's throat and making her eyes itch.

The alcove in the crypts was empty, save for the IV rack dangling from the ceiling, the chains bolted to the wall, and an impressive pile of ash formerly known as Renault Duchanes.

"How the *fuck* did this happen?" Gabriel demanded.

"Suicide," Colin said.

Gabriel toed the pile of ash. "By what means? He would've needed a stake, or hellfire, or—"

"Decapitation. Look at the chains," Colin said, pointing out the one that'd bound Renault's wrists, the iron links coated in so much ash it was nearly white. Colin looped it around his neck, mimicking a noose. "It would've been the only way."

"You're telling me the vampire Jacinda and I beat and

tortured—the vampire we left bleeding to death and barely conscious—had the strength to wrap an iron chain around his neck so tightly he cut off his own head?" Gabriel let out a bitter laugh. "Forgive me for questioning your professional assessment, Dr. Redthorne, but that's just not possible."

"Fucking coward." Dorian paced the small space of the alcove. Then, whirling on Colin and Aiden, "You two were supposed to be monitoring him. How could he have done something like this without your knowledge?"

"We were in Father's laboratory on the other side of the crypts," Colin said. "I'd only just changed his IV bags moments earlier. He must've done it right after I left. I'm sorry, Dorian. If I'd known it was possible for him to—"

"It *wasn't* possible." Jaci ran her fingers along the cold stone wall, trying not to lose the last of her dwindling hope. Renault was a piece of utter garbage, but he was also the vampire with the magic heart—the heart that was supposed to bind Viansa, help break the Redthorne curse, and stop a dastardly demonic plot from destroying the entire world. "You don't smell the brimstone? This wasn't a suicide. It was a demon attack."

"*Viansa*," Gabriel gritted out. "Is she here?"

"Not physically, no. I think she just… got into his head."

"And convinced him to chop it off?"

"She must've figured out we'd taken him hostage," Jaci said. "Maybe he even told her as much, hoping she could bust him out. Stupid asshole. He was no good to her as a Redthorne prisoner."

"Now he's no good to us either. *Fuck*!" Gabriel grabbed the chains, tore them right from the stone. Chunks of rock and metal hit the ground, a crack splitting the wall.

"Gabriel," Jaci said.

No response.

"*Gabriel*."

He spun around to face her, frustration and anger drawing his face tight. "Duchanes was our best shot at—"

His words fell away, and in an instant, all that rage turned into pure, uncut pain. She saw it slice through his eyes, heard it in the sharp and sudden gasp he sucked through his teeth.

"Jacinda!" he hissed. "Get… out of here. *Go!*"

Without warning, Dorian grabbed her and shoved her against the stone wall, shielding her with his body as Gabriel barreled into him from behind. Fangs bared, his irises a deadly shade of red, he shoved past Dorian's arm and wrapped a hand around Jaci's throat.

Not in the sexy way.

"It's… Viansa," Gabriel ground out, shaking with the effort of holding the succubus at bay. "In my… head. You… danger. I can't…"

His face twisted, lips drawing back over his fangs, eyes full of so much malice she hardly recognized him as the man who claimed to love her.

Dorian finally managed to loosen Gabriel's grip, then tore him away from her, slamming him into the opposite wall and shouting for Jaci to get the fuck out of there.

But she wouldn't leave him. Not like this.

Dorian had one side of him pinned against the stone wall, Aiden jumping in on the other, both of them scrambling to keep the savage vampire in check.

"Listen to me, Gabriel," Jaci said softly. "You can fight her. You *have* to fight her. Don't give in."

She watched the struggle play out across his face, pain and fury, fear and frustration, his body trembling beneath Dorian and Aiden's hold.

And then, as suddenly as the terror had begun, it was over.

Like a balloon poked with a pin, Gabriel deflated, all of the violence draining away as he sighed and slumped forward into Dorian's arms.

"Holy shit," Charley whispered, and all Jaci could do was nod. It'd all happened so fast… Viansa had slipped through the protective magic, hijacking Gabriel's mind and…

She closed her eyes, relief flooding her limbs. It could've been worse. So much worse.

"Everyone okay?" Isabelle asked. "Gabriel? Are you hurt?"

Gabriel shook his head, and Dorian finally released him.

But then Gabriel's eyes went wide with some new fear, and he dropped into a crouch, narrowly ducking the fist that rocketed into the wall above his head.

Dorian's fist.

"Fuck! The bitch is still here!" Gabriel grabbed Dorian's legs and dropped his ass to the ground, and the two vampires wrestled for control, snapping and growling, fangs tearing through clothes and flesh as they fought like feral cats.

Amidst a flurry of shouts and blurs, Cole, Aiden, and Charley tried in vain to wrest Dorian and Gabriel apart, but the two vampires wouldn't let up. Jaci had no idea whether Viansa was still in Dorian's head or whether she'd jumped back into Gabriel's, but one thing was clear—if they didn't stop her, soon they'd be Hoovering up more than just Renault's ashes.

"Do something!" Jaci shouted, but who the hell was she talking to? What could anyone do against an invisible enemy who could break into their heads without warning, turning them all into monsters?

"Jacinda." Isabelle grabbed Jaci's arm, her voice low and urgent. "I've got an idea. Buy me some time."

"How much?"

"As much as you can." Isabelle slipped away, disappearing down the tunnel that led back to Augustus Redthorne's old laboratory.

"Viansa!" Jaci held up her palms, calling twin bursts of hellfire to life. "Time to fight your own battles, you coward. Show yourself!"

The vampires were on their feet now, Gabriel dodging a blow to the jaw. With a vicious bite, he tore a chunk out of Dorian's shoulder, blood spraying across his face.

The wound healed at once, and Dorian cocked his arm back for another blow.

"Show yourself, succubus!" Jaci unleashed a surge of hellfire just over their heads, and the vampires ducked, narrowly avoiding the scorching silver flames. When they rose to their full heights again, their eyes were clear, the bloodlust that had overtaken them all but gone.

"Did she… Did she leave?" Gabriel panted, dragging the back of his hand across his bloody mouth. "Is that fucking succubus gone?"

"Hell no," came the chipper reply—this time, from Charley. "Why would I leave when the party's just getting good?"

"Charlotte!" Dorian swept her into his arms, wrapping her in such a tight hold, she could barely move. "Fight her, love," he said. "You're a lot stronger than she is."

"Am I?" Charley laughed, cold and cruel, but then Viansa jumped again—Cole.

He snarled and dropped to the ground, his muscles twisting and bunching, bones popping as he shifted into his wolf form. Gabriel and Dorian jumped on top of him, Gabriel pinning him down while Dorian fought to hold his snapping jaw shut.

"What do we do?" Gabriel asked. "What the hell do we do?"

Cole finally stopped struggling, and the bitch was on the move once more. Aiden was the next target. He blurred at Gabriel, smashing his fist into Gabriel's gut, then blurring into Colin, taking him down with a mean uppercut.

Before Colin could even retaliate, Viansa jumped back to Charley. Back to Aiden. Dorian. Cole, still in his wolf form.

Hellfire surging in her palms, Jaci watched in helpless agony as her sister swept through the group like a raging virus. They couldn't catch her, couldn't force her out, couldn't risk wounding her.

Couldn't do a fucking thing but wait.

"Viansa," Jaci tried again. "What do you want? I said I'd help you with the hell gates, but I can't do *shit* if you won't talk to me. Stop fucking around and face me like a real demon. Now!"

Viansa's shrill, earsplitting laugh pierced the air, but it hadn't come from any of the group. Jaci couldn't even place the source—the succubus was nowhere and everywhere all at once. Taunting them. Surrounding them.

"Fuck this," Gabriel said. "Time to go." He grabbed Jaci's arm, tried to move her down the tunnel, but they'd only managed to take a few steps before Viansa jumped again, this time returning to Colin.

With a wild roar, Colin blurred into them both, the impact knocking Jaci on her ass. She heard Dorian shouting at Colin to stop, heard the snarl of Cole's wolf, heard Gabriel cry out in such deep, all-encompassing agony, Jaci was terrified to look. Terrified she'd find him mangled and mutilated, seconds from turning into ash.

When she finally got to her feet and got her bearings, Colin had Gabriel against the cracked stone wall, one arm against his throat, his fist embedded in Gabriel's chest.

The crypts fell silent, the splash of Gabriel's blood on the floor and the pounding of Jaci's own frantic heartbeat the only sounds that reached her.

Dorian was the first to speak. The only one who dared.

"Colin," he said gently. Desperately. Tears glazed his eyes, but he kept his voice steady. "Don't give in, brother. Please."

"I love it when you beg, vampire king," Colin said. Rather, it was Colin's voice, but it wasn't *him*. Wasn't his face. Wasn't his warm, compassionate eyes and sweet dimples.

In that moment, Colin wore the mask of a monster.

"Yeah, I'm kinda bored of this game anyway," the monster said. "Time to end—"

"No," Jaci gasped, and the gleam in Colin's monster-eyes confirmed her worst fear.

Viansa was going to kill Gabriel.

"Whatever you want," Jaci whispered, too petrified to move. To even cry. "I'm right here, Viansa. I'm all yours. Just don't—"

"Why not?" Colin snapped, his voice high and tight. "You took *my* vampire. Maybe I'll take yours. Only fair, right?"

"Or *maybe*," came another reply, sharp and clear, "we'll send you back to hell and call it a day."

Isabelle.

The witch hurled a glass jar at Colin's feet. It shattered with an explosion of indigo light, magic sizzling along the ground and racing up the stone walls, enveloping Colin and Gabriel in a cloud of smoke.

Jaci felt Viansa's dark energy scatter. A flood of shock

and confusion, a spike of sheer terror, the overwhelming desire to flee, and then... Nothing but lightness in the air. Room to breathe.

By the time the smoke faded, the bitch was completely gone.

"Gabriel," Jaci whispered, and across the broken, blood-stained alcove, the vampire prince caught her gaze and smiled.

Keeping his eyes and Jaci, he said, "So, Colin... I don't suppose you might... I don't know. Unhand my *fucking* heart? Preferably while it's still beating?"

Colin gasped, blinking in disbelief as his awareness finally returned and he took in the gruesome sight.

"Colin," Gabriel said again, softer now. "Are you with me?"

"I... Yes. I'm... so sorry, brother. This is... quite unexpected."

"Quite uncomfortable as well." Gabriel grinned, clearly trying to put on a brave face. "No sudden movements, Dr. Redthorne. Surgical precision, yes?"

"Of course," Colin said, clearing his throat. "Of course." Slowly, painstakingly, he released Gabriel's heart and withdrew his fist.

Collapsing back against the wall, Gabriel unleashed a sigh that quickly turned into a relieved laugh, and Jaci watched in awe as the mangled hole in his chest closed, flesh and bone knitting back together as if someone had just hit the rewind button on the whole gruesome scene.

By the time he stood up and pulled Jaci into an impossibly tight embrace, the only evidence that he'd been attacked at all was the ragged hole torn through his shirt, the pool of blood still glistening at his feet.

The flick of a Zippo, the suck-and-crackle of a cigarette, and they all turned to see Cole in the shadow of the alcove, stark naked and covered in blood and dirt, his clothing in tattered rags at his feet.

"You good, wolf?" Gabriel asked with a laugh. "You look a bit… bedraggled."

"Like I said." Cole took a long, deep, drag, then blew it out slowly. "Anytime you Redthornes are ready to pack it in on the supernatural shitshow, I got yer backs. Team Regular Family Bullshit, at your service."

"I'll see about ordering some matching T-shirts," Aiden said.

"Flamethrowers," Cole said. "Much more practical for this fucking bunch. Now if you'll excuse me, I've got a date with my bed and an entire brick of Mary Jane guaran-damn-*teed* to wipe the last two days outta my memory, and I don't wanna hear another word from *any* of you tonight unless you got a lead on some cheap American whiskey, a beautiful woman lookin' to make an honest man outta me, or…" He narrowed his eyes and took another drag, then shook his head. "Nope. That's all I got."

"Whiskey and women," Dorian said as they watched the retreating form of Cole's bare ass disappear into the darkness. "Looks like the wolf is back to his old self—no permanent damage done."

Jaci wanted to laugh, but couldn't. One look at the Redthorne vampires, and she saw the horrible truth flashing through their eyes like a blazing neon sign.

The permanent damage was all theirs.

And it was about to hit every one of them, hard and fast.

CHAPTER ELEVEN

The Redthornes were exhausted.

For the past few weeks, they'd done a bang-up job pretending otherwise, but when they left the crypts and the adrenaline rush finally subsided, not a single one of those broody, commanding vampires could keep up the act.

The curse was tearing them apart inside, and the battle with Viansa had taken a heavy toll—mentally *and* physically.

They were back in the kitchen, once again gathered around the breakfast nook. Only now, there were no stacks of rich, buttery pancakes, no coffee cups waiting for a refill, no piles of crispy, cooked-to-perfection bacon.

Just blood.

Bottles and bags of it, most of Dorian's on-hand supply spread out on the table as Jaci and Isabelle triaged the rapidly weakening vampires. Dorian and Gabriel were the worst off, so shockingly pale they looked like wraiths. By the time Jaci had gotten them situated in their chairs, they could barely hold up their own heads.

Colin was in slightly better shape, but he still needed four bottles of blood before he could even speak again. And Charley and Aiden, who'd yet to show any definitive signs of the curse, were suddenly overcome with ravenous hunger and a painful sensitivity to the daylight that had Isabelle scrambling to draw the blinds.

Whether it was the fight with Viansa, the curse finally knocking them for a loop, or something else entirely, Jaci couldn't be sure.

All she knew was they needed blood. A lot of it—and fast.

She and Isabelle worked in silence, clearing away the old bottles as quickly as they passed out new ones, keeping a close eye on the vampires for signs of further deterioration as they sucked down bottle after bottle, bag after bag.

Twenty minutes later, the vampires were finally showing signs of life again, the color returning to their faces, the conversation picking up where they'd left off in the crypts, all of them trying to figure out what to do about Viansa—especially now that they'd lost Renault's heart.

"That potion," Jaci said, rinsing out a few bottles and passing them to Isabelle. "I've never seen anything like it. I could literally *feel* Viansa fleeing the scene. It reminded me of shining a flashlight on a bunch of cockroaches."

"That's precisely the idea." Isabelle arranged the clean bottles in the drying rack on the counter. "Think of it like a magical flash-bang. Liquid explosives inside a glass receptacle, both charged with devil's trap sigils."

Jaci laughed. "And Aiden thinks *I'm* spooky."

"You are spooky," Aiden said. "Both of you. Think I'll start referring to you as the Spooky Sisters."

"How does that even work, though?" Charley asked. "I get that a regular devil's trap sigil—like, the ones you paint on the ground—can trap demonic essences. But liquid splatters everywhere—doesn't that just dilute the effect?"

"Yes, and that's precisely why it worked," Isabelle said. "Viansa is an original demon. A devil's trap could never hold someone so powerful, but it can still cause a visceral reaction to the perceived danger. When this one blew, it scattered the trap over a wide area, sending her essence into sensory overload. She couldn't tell where the threat was coming from, so she panicked and fled. Self-perseveration at its finest."

"Brilliant," Dorian said.

"Maybe so," Isabelle said, drying her hands on a dishtowel and joining them at the table. "But it's not a permanent solution. She'll be back as soon as she regroups and realizes the threat's gone."

"Can you make more?" Gabriel asked.

"It's my top priority now that you're out of the woods. But…" She looked at Jaci across the kitchen, her face tight with worry. "We need to figure out that binding spell. We've managed to hold off the worst of her attacks, but she's getting stronger. Today proved as much. We almost lost…" She trailed off and lowered her eyes.

Jaci nodded, grateful Isabelle hadn't said Gabriel's name out loud.

Remembering that desperate look in his eyes, the pain in his voice, the sight of Colin's fist wrapped around Gabriel's heart…

No. If she thought about it for too long, she'd break. And right now, she couldn't afford to break. Not with so many lives on the line. So much at stake.

"We don't even know where Viansa's physical body is," Gabriel said. "And with Duchanes gone, we've lost our main ingredient for that binding spell."

"We'll find something else," Isabelle said sternly. "We don't have a choice."

"Colin," Aiden said, "any ideas from a medical perspective? Can we remove just *part* of a cursed vampire's heart without killing him outright?"

"You volunteering, Aiden?" Gabriel laughed. "Might as well remove part of your brain while he's got you under the knife. Clearly, you're not using it—won't even miss it, I'm betting."

"No one is going under the knife," Colin said. "It's too risky, even for a vampire. Our hearts function like human hearts. You can't just take a little off the top without risking a serious injury—one that could prove fatal, even to a vampire."

"What if we sire a new vampire?" Gabriel asked. "Expressly for this purpose."

"You're not serious," Dorian said.

"Why the hell not?" Gabriel shrugged. "We carry the

curse, right? Pass it on to any vampire we sire. So let's just find some degenerate human who deserves to—"

"*No*," Dorian said. "Turning humans into test subjects without their consent? Then we're no better than the filthy demons who trick them into selling their souls for—" Dorian cut off abruptly, then glanced over at Jaci, offering an awkward smile. "Sorry. I didn't mean—"

"Hey, I almost killed you, remember?" Jaci leaned back against the sink and laughed. "The way I see it, you've earned at least a dozen more insults before we're even."

Dorian nodded, his smile relaxing into something a little less strained. "Noted."

"Dorian's right, guys," Charley said. "We can't just make a new vampire, and obviously none of us is volunteering for surgery. Face it—Operation Heart Donor is dead. We need a plan B."

"Plan *D*," Gabriel said. "Degenerate. You're all dismissing the idea far too quickly."

"Easy there, killer." Aiden picked up a rogue blueberry and chucked it at Gabriel's head. "Isn't there a family of deer out back you can slaughter to relieve your murderous urges?"

"Don't you have a teenager to impress?" Gabriel chucked the blueberry right back. "Go make her a mixtape or something."

"Mixtape?" Aiden cracked up. "What century do you think this is, Grandpa?"

Colin's phone buzzed, and he excused himself to take the call in the dining room, the rest of them trading barbs and laughing at Gabriel and Aiden's antics while Jaci chewed on her thumbnail, mind racing for that elusive plan B.

A blood curse bound in darkness.

Fight like with like.

No heart, no spell.

Viansa's magic.

Hell's magic.

Like with like.

Viansa.

Jacinda.

Hell…

"It's me," she finally said, the realization slamming straight into her chest. "It has to be me."

The room fell silent, all of them looking up at her as if she'd finally lost it.

Hell, maybe she had. But they were out of time. Out of options.

Survival mode—engaged.

"*What* has to be you?" Gabriel asked, his green eyes fiery.

"We don't need a heart, Prince. We don't need another vampire. We just need me. I'm your plan B."

"You?" The ground beneath her feet practically rumbled with the force of Gabriel's ridiculous laughter. "I think the fuck *not*."

"Now who's being dismissive, Prince?"

"Jacinda, we're not risking your life just to—"

"Just to what?" She paced the kitchen, anger simmering

inside. "Save the people I care about? Break this curse before it breaks you?"

"Forget the curse," Gabriel said. "We've lived with it for two hundred fifty years. We're not fucking off just yet."

"Look around you, Prince." Jaci gestured at the table still littered with spent blood bags. "How much longer do you think you've got? Not another two centuries—I'll tell you that much."

"We'll figure something out," he said.

"That's what this is. Me, figuring something else out." She dropped into the chair next to him, taking his hands in hers. "I'm not giving up on this. On you. Just because we don't have Renault's heart doesn't mean we can't fix it. It just means it's going to be a little more—"

"Dangerous," Gabriel said, at the same time Aiden said, "Impossible."

"*Complicated*," Jaci said. "And, yeah, fine. Maybe a little dangerous, but when has that *ever* stopped anyone in this house?"

Gabriel sighed. "Jacinda, I appreciate what you're saying, but—"

"One time," she said, getting to her feet again. "Give me one time when any one of you turned your back on something just because it was dangerous. Or impossible for that matter. You're fucking vampires! I'm a witch-demon hybrid freak. Our very *existence* is supposed to be impossible, yet here we are, *existing*. So unless one of you can honestly tell me you're ready to walk away from this fight without trying every crazy, impossible, risky, Hail Mary, suicide-mission idea we can conjure, I'm not ruling out a *damn* thing."

Silence.

She'd rendered them speechless.

"The overall strategy hasn't changed," she continued. "We bind Viansa's powers and trap her here, forcing her to confess the location of my father's soul. Once I've rescued him, we can take her out for good."

"She dies, her magic dies," Charley said. "Her magic dies, the curse is broken."

Jaci nodded. "The binding itself is the most important step. Originally, my theory was that a Redthorne heart— a heart tainted by the very curse my sister bound with her dark magic—was the key to counteracting that dark magic and stripping her powers."

"A connection forged by a certain magic can also be broken by that same magic when that magic is intentionally altered for a different purpose," Gabriel said, repeating the explanation she'd given him when she'd first confessed about the heart. "That's what you said. Fight like with like."

"Exactly."

"But we don't have the heart." Gabriel scrubbed a hand over his face and groaned. "We're going in bloody circles."

"The curse inside you isn't Viansa's only dark creation," Jaci said softly.

They all looked up at her again, and she lifted her eyebrows, waiting for them to put the pieces together.

"You don't mean…" Gabriel closed his eyes, his voice

dropping to a whisper. "When you said we just need *you*, you meant that quite literally."

"I don't know why I didn't think of it before. I'm her dark creation, guys. Me. My very existence. Viansa calls me Lab Rat because that's exactly what I am—her magical science project. The living, breathing result of her and my mother's hell magic—the darkest power you can imagine."

Jaci felt that dark power surge inside her now, hot and furious. It made her blood sing, her heart skip, her whole body spring-loaded and ready to fight. To break. To fucking *destroy*.

"The key to the binding spell lies somewhere inside of you," Isabelle said, meeting Jaci's gaze. Her lips curved into a smile, and Jaci nodded, a new understanding passing between them.

They were going to figure out that spell.

And they were going to put Viansa in the fucking *ground*.

Gabriel opened his mouth to say something to her, but then his gaze shifted behind her, his brow tightening with new worry. "Colin? What's wrong?"

"That was the hospital calling," Colin said. "They've just discovered thirteen more victims of a ritual killing in Chelsea. This time, one of them actually survived."

"Holy shit," Jaci said. "Is she talking?"

Colin shook his head, his mouth pulled into a deep frown. "I'm sorry—I have to go. They need a pediatric surgical consult."

"Pediatric?" Jaci asked, unable to hide the horror in her voice.

"The victim is eleven years old. They don't expect she'll survive the night, but we have to try." Colin let out a deep sigh. "I'll be back as soon as I can. Oh, and Jacinda? Whatever you and Isabelle decide about this spell—count me in."

"Count us *all* in," Dorian said, and Charley and Aiden nodded.

When she met Gabriel's eyes again, she saw the concern behind them, but there was pride too. Love. And a fierce, unwavering loyalty that bolstered her like nothing else could.

"Partners," he said with a soft smile, all for her. "Always."

"Best put on the kettle, Jacinda." Isabelle rose from her chair and picked up the last of the discarded blood bags. "The Spooky Sisters have got our work cut out for us tonight."

CHAPTER TWELVE

"To my good friends, Dorian and Gabriel Redthorne." Alexei Rogozin lifted his glass of vodka, nodding at the vampires seated across from him in the Ravenswood dining room. "And to wolf, who looks like he tried to piss on angry grizzly bear."

Cole, who'd returned to Ravenswood for the late-night meeting only after Dorian convinced him expensive Russian vodka was close enough to cheap American whiskey to warrant the trip, grinned. "Don't be jealous of the scars, Mr. Rogozin. I know a guy who can hook you up for the right price."

"That is hard pass from me," he said with a laugh. "This face? Smooth as baby's bottom."

"The offer stands." Cole touched the rim of his glass to Rogozin's. Then, they drank.

Ever the diplomat, Dorian made a show of gushing

about the vodka Rogozin had brought, but Gabriel felt no such compulsions.

Vodka only reminded him of Shimmer—a place he was still trying to forget.

Leaving his drink untouched, he said, "Alexei, I understand my brother has informed you about a hellspawn—"

Dorian kicked him under the table.

"Forgive me," Gabriel continued, forcing a smile for his brother's sake. "A *demonic* problem we've stumbled into. We were hoping we might consult with you about the best course of action."

Rogozin took another sip of his vodka, then nodded. "I am honored to offer my counsel to House Redthorne."

"And we're honored to receive it, as always," Dorian said.

At that, Gabriel finally tossed back a swig of vodka, barely hiding his scowl.

Bloody hell, the pomp and circumstance. And these were the leaders of the two most powerful supernatural factions in New York? It was a wonder they got anything accomplished at all, what with all the mutual dick-stroking going on.

"Gabriel?" Dorian said. "Would you like to fill Alexei in on what we've discovered?"

No, brother. I'd like to be upstairs in your guest room, balls deep in my witch as she rakes her nails down my back and begs me not to stop, but apparently, that's too much to ask…

Another kick to the shin. An icy glare. A deep, disappointed sigh.

For fuck's sake.

Clearing his throat, Gabriel looked at Rogozin again and said, "An original demon has manifested here—a succubus. It appears she's working with a group of dark mages called the Keepers of the Dark Flame to permanently destroy the hell gates."

"An original succubus?" Rogozin asked.

"The original succubus." Gabriel took another sip of vodka, forcing himself not to grimace. "She and the mages are responsible for a number of ritual murders in the city —*human* murders—committed so they might harness the death energy that allows the succubus to grow more powerful and maintain her position outside of hell."

"To what end?" he asked.

"We believe the group intends on creating a permanent, unrestricted passageway between our realms, allowing demons to bypass the laws of the Shadow Accords and manifest here at will. Ultimately, they're plotting to overthrow the established supernatural communities and claim the earthly realm as their domain."

"Demons. Never satisfied with station in life." Rogozin blew out a breath, then reached for the bottle of vodka and topped off all of their glasses, filling his own nearly to the rim. "Unrestricted demon highway… Bad for business. *My* business."

"Some of them are likely already here," Gabriel said. Careful not to reveal Jacinda's name—or their relationship —or that fact that she was in that very manor at that very moment—he said, "One of our associates familiar with succubus lore told us that such demons often initiate sexual encounters with humans in order to breed demon-human hybrids."

Rogozin nodded. "I've heard of such practices, but I've not met any of these hybrids personally."

"You may not have realized it if you *had* met one," Gabriel continued. "These hybrids can allegedly pass between our realm and hell at will, and can exist here as is, no human vessels required. To most of us, they'd appear human—an advantage that allows them to hide in plain sight."

"Hide from what?" Rogozin asked. "What is advantage, exactly?"

"Are you familiar with the term 'sleeper cell?'"

Rogozin's face paled. "You think hybrids here are just… just waiting for call to arms?"

"I think it's entirely possible given what we know about the demon behind all of this."

"The succubus," he said. "She is commander?"

"That's what we thought initially, but no. Looks like she's just following orders."

Rogozin closed his eyes and sighed heavily through his nose. He seemed to be collecting his thoughts. Weighing his options.

When he glanced up at Gabriel again, his face was even more grim than before. "Azerius. That is why you called me here. You believe he is behind plot."

Gabriel nodded. "Apparently, the prospect of a thousand-year banishment in hell isn't sitting well with him. He wants out."

"And you are certain your succubus is working for him? Working to bring him here?"

"Certain? No," Gabriel said. "But it's a *very* strong possibility—one we must give serious consideration."

"Our source on that particular matter was unreliable at best," Dorian said, "but also in no position to lie about it."

"Was?" Rogozin asked. "Source is… past tense? Who?"

Gabriel looked at Dorian, who nodded for him to continue.

"Renault Duchanes," Gabriel said.

Rogozin arched an eyebrow. "You found vampire traitor?"

"We captured him from a warehouse in New Jersey where he'd been working to amass a supernatural army of sorts," Gabriel said. "We'd hoped to learn more about his plans and their connection to the demonic plot, but he was killed by the succubus just this morning."

He relayed the story of Viansa's hit-and-run, then filled him in about what they'd discovered at the warehouse, once again leaving Jacinda's identity out of it.

"Duchanes ain't the only one playing Dr. Frankenstein, either," Cole said when Gabriel had finished up. "One of my guys checked in earlier. They're still tracking grays in the woods all over the region. Got some new reports of shifters gone missing—all males, all from further upstate and into Vermont."

"Missing?" Gabriel asked. This was the first he'd heard of more shifter abductions.

"Nabbed right outta their beds, according to their family members." Cole scratched his beard, trying but failing to hold back a shudder. "Evidence of silver poisoning."

Gabriel's gut twisted. He could only imagine what the wolf had endured in captivity. He'd hoped they'd seen the last of those particular experiments when he'd killed the poor beasts trapped in the warehouse cages, but it seemed that wasn't the case.

Fucking Duchanes. Death was too good for you…

"There's a good chance whoever's releasing the grays and kidnapping the shifters is a follower of Duchanes," he said to Cole now. "Based on the numbers you gave me after your initial recon, I'd say we took down less than a third of them at the warehouse."

"Figured as much about the mages," Cole said. "I counted at least a hundred that first day. You took out, what?"

"Two dozen at most."

"Math ain't my strong suit, but… yeah." Cole nodded. "Still a bunch more unaccounted for. And those fuckers sure seem happy to carry on the tradition of torturing my people."

"And *we'll* happily carry on the tradition of sending every last one of them to hell," Gabriel said.

"Assuming we can find 'em." Cole slid a cigarette from his pack, tapped it against the table. "I know Duchanes said he was preppin' for some kinda war, but I'm not so sure about all that. From what I saw on the inside? He was just a cowardly bloodsucker stacking the deck, waiting to see which faction would come out on top so he could slide right in. All those monsters he created, all those mages... They were always gonna pick the winning side."

"Common strategy among lesser men." Rogozin hissed into his vodka. "Where is loyalty? Where is sense of honor?"

"You won't find either among the followers of Renault Duchanes," Dorian said. Then, to Cole, "Given what you saw at the warehouse, do you believe Duchanes was doing all of this to help Azerius, or to take a stand against him?"

"Help," Cole said. "His money was *always* on Azerius. Azerius and Viansa—that's the winning ticket right there."

"I understand the connection between Azerius, Viansa, and the mages," Dorian said, gazing into his half-empty glass. "They're working together to break down the hell gates and give Azerius enough power to leave hell and take his true form in our realm. But the other supernaturals, the experiments... It almost seems beneath him. What does Azerius want with a bunch of mangled grays and resurrected shifters? Even the demons and vampires on Duchanes' payroll were low-level henchmen, easily replaced."

"Someone to fight his battles," Rogozin said. "All-powerful demon lord such as Azerius... He does not want to get hands dirty. To him, other supernaturals are..." He rubbed his fingers together, searching for the word. "...expendable."

"He's not merely looking to overthrow our rule here," Gabriel said, a few more of the pieces sliding into place. "He wants to turn our realm into a demonic realm. An *entirely* demonic realm. "

"Hell 2.0?" Rogozin laughed, but the punchline was utterly lost on Gabriel.

"Forgive me, Alexei, but do you think this is funny?"

"Gabriel," Dorian warned. "Let's not insult our guest. He's only trying to lighten the mood."

"We're talking about an apocalyptic event, Dorian. There's no lightening *that* mood." Gabriel rose from his chair, paced the dining room. Dorian could play politics all he wanted, but Gabriel was damn near crawling out of his mind trying to figure this thing out.

Azerius. Viansa. Keepers of the Dark Flame. Demon-human hybrids.

It was one thing for them to take out the royal vampires and assert themselves as leaders of the supernatural world —after all, that's why Viansa and her mother had bred Jacinda, hoping to create an even more powerful hybrid than the ones the succubi could offer.

But turning the earthly realm into a second hell? That was bloody terrifying.

"Think about it, Dorian," Gabriel said. "What is hell but a prison for banished souls? A place where the most powerful demons have free reign—*sanctioned* reign—to eternally torture and brutalize the souls of every human and supernatural who ends up there?"

"What are you getting at?" Dorian asked, a flicker of concern finally flashing through his eyes.

"If Azerius and Viansa rise to power in the material realm, take out vampires and the rest of the supernaturals in their way, and create a second hell, then *every* remaining soul on this planet immediately becomes part of hell's domain—not just the souls who've earned the trip there."

"You're talking about an eternal torture chamber," Dorian said. "The demonic enslavement of every being on this planet."

Gabriel gave him a sarcastic grin. "Is your mood lighter yet, brother?"

"Hell 2.0 ain't gonna happen," Cole said adamantly. "Not as long as I'm still breathing."

Dorian plucked the cigarette from between Cole's lips and broke it. "Let's not tempt fate, shall we?"

"We need to go after Azerius," Gabriel said. "Viansa's our first priority, but he *has* to be next."

"But if we eliminate Viansa," Dorian said, "Azerius has no way to manifest here. He's depending on her to see this through."

"Yes, until she fucks off into the sunset and the next original demon moves up the ranks, all too happy to plant his lips on the King of Blood and Ravens' all-powerful arse."

Rogozin set his glass down hard on the table, spearing Gabriel with an icy glare.

"Apologies if I've offended you," Gabriel said, "but

you'd be a fool to assume your hellspawn origin grants you immunity from a demonic tyrant."

"*Gabriel*," Dorian hissed, but Gabriel was far from finished.

He was just getting started.

"He Who Drinks the Blood of the Fallen," he continued. "That's what they call him. He Whom Before All Mortals Weep. He Who Slaughters the Blood of his Blood. Azerius murdered his own siblings, for fuck's sake. What makes you think he gives a fuck about you?" Gabriel stopped pacing and leaned forward, hands braced on the table, unflinching in the face of Rogozin's mounting anger. "Your organization may be the most powerful demonic faction in this realm, Alexei, but with all due respect, you're *not* originals. You're not even ancients. Unless you can prove yourselves critical and irreplaceable, you'll find yourselves weeping before the King of Blood and Bullshit just like the rest of us, and on that day, I want you to remember this moment. Remember that the vampire prince was the one who warned you of your demise when all others sought only to placate you."

Rogozin stared at him for a long moment, fingers tight around his glass, eyes narrowed, assessing.

Gabriel had to give the man credit. He didn't erupt. Didn't roast Gabriel in a ball of hellfire. Didn't demand an explanation from Dorian for his little brother's outburst.

He just waited. Watched. Considered.

Gabriel didn't flinch either, though he was starting to understand why Dorian wanted the demon on their side.

For all Gabriel's doubts, Rogozin was a formidable player. Whether he could be trusted or not was immaterial; Dorian was wise to keep him close.

But Gabriel was formidable too. Had been since the day his bastard of a father had taught him the hard lessons about mercy and weakness. Jacinda may have melted the ice from his heart, but he had a *lifetime* of reserves saved up for just such an occasion as exterminating a nefarious demonic turncoat at the first hint of subterfuge…

"You have valid point, vampire prince," Rogozin finally said, lowering his eyes and returning his attention to his drink. "Maybe work on delivery, though."

He laughed, but once again, the humor was lost on Gabriel

"So you agree Azerius needs to be eliminated?" Gabriel pressed. "And you'll help us with this?"

Glaring at Gabriel once more, Rogozin reached for the bottle, emptying the last of it into his glass. After a deep drink, he said, "Azerius is complicated situation. Taking stand against him… It is forbidden by sacred oath."

"You've got to be kidding me."

Rogozin set down his glass and rolled up his sleeve, revealing the white raven tattooed on his inner forearm. It shimmered eerily in the light, the sight of it sending an unexpected chill down Gabriel's spine.

"Some oaths," Gabriel said, finally reclaiming his chair, "no matter how sacred, must be broken."

"Some, yes. This one? Not so simple." He pushed his sleeve back into place. "This isn't just tattoo from corner shop. This is dark magic. Sacred promise. Bound by hell's most—"

Gabriel held up a hand, cutting him off. He'd heard enough about dark magical binds and all the ways hell had conspired to fuck the entire world.

"So you're saying none of the Rogozin demons can help with this?" Gabriel asked. "Because of your sacred oath?"

"Rogozin demons aren't the only ones who venerate Azerius, Gabriel," Dorian said. "Many of the other factions in this city have sworn fealty to him."

Rogozin nodded. "This is true. However, I did not say we can't help. Only that we can't take stand."

Gabriel shot Dorian a glance, but the vampire king seemed content to let the princeling fight the good fight.

I will kick your arse later, Gabriel mouthed.

Then, to Rogozin, "You can't take a stand? What does that mean, exactly?"

Rogozin tipped back his glass. Drained it. Tried for another go at the gold medal in their staring contest.

When it was clear Gabriel wouldn't back down, Rogozin finally said, "I know you don't always agree with our methods, vampire prince. And is clear you dislike me, despite my allegiance to your family."

"Alexei," Dorian said, "I can assure you, Gabriel is—"

Rogozin held up his hand. "I understand. I had brother once too. But prince—Gabriel—believe me when I tell you my organization wants peace. We want to work in this city, to exist below radar of human authorities. We do not wish to bring wars of underworld into streets of New York."

"On that, we are absolutely aligned," Dorian said, and Gabriel nodded.

"You have plan for dealing with succubus?" Rogozin asked.

"We are working with dark witches on a spell that will bind her power and keep her trapped here long enough for us to eliminate her," Dorian said, thankfully leaving out the part about rescuing Jacinda's father from hell. "But our witches have not yet perfected the spell."

Rogozin nodded. "I do not know about magic and binding spells—that is witch's domain. But I do know way to kill original demon like Viansa."

"What about Azerius?" Gabriel pressed.

"I told you, vampire prince. Those who've sworn fealty to King of Ravens cannot actively take up arms against him."

"But—"

"*But* to leave something is very different from taking something, yes?"

Gabriel reined in the urge to ask him if he was drunk. "I don't understand, Alexei. Leave something?"

"Taking, leaving, it is all matter of interpretation." He rose from his chair, lifting the small black briefcase he'd carried in with him. Then, setting it on the table, he said, "I am old. Not ancient, as you helpfully reminded me, but old. Memory is… unreliable. Sometimes I forget things. I leave them behind. Sometimes others find these things. Sometimes they remember conversations that I, being an old demon who is fond of vodka, do not."

Cole—clearly fluent in the language of the perpetually inebriated—nodded sagely, but Gabriel was lost. He understood that Alexei meant to leave the briefcase behind, but he couldn't make heads or tails of the man's cryptic babble.

"Thank you for enlightening evening," Rogozin said with a smile that appeared genuine. Then, turning to Gabriel, "And for honesty. When we meet again, perhaps we will drink to surviving King of Blood and Bullshit, yes?"

Gabriel had no idea what the hell to say to all that, so he just nodded and reached out to shake Alexei's hand.

The demon said his farewells, then saw himself out.

After replacing the vodka with scotch and bourbon— and Cole's favorite cheap whiskey—Dorian finally opened the briefcase.

"Bloody fucking hell," he whispered.

"*That* old thing?" Cole shook his head. "And here I thought he was leaving us some of them Russian dolls or more vodka or… something."

Dorian flipped the case around so Gabriel could see it.

His stomach bottomed out at the sight. "Is that…"

"The Blade of Azerius," Dorian said.

Gabriel stared in utter disbelief.

Nestled into the velvet-lined case was a bone-handled dagger with a blade cut like a raven's wing—a blade as magical as it was ancient.

It was a weapon with the ability to strip a demonic essence from its human vessel with a single nick, trapping it for eternity inside the blade itself, never to re-spawn, never to awaken. The effect on humans was equally dire, expelling a human soul straight to hell, turning the body into a vessel ripe for demonic possession.

It was the weapon Dorian had shoved into Malcolm's chest at Bloodbath, saving Charlotte's life and inadvertently summoning Azerius himself—one more falling domino in the chain that eventually led to Malcolm's brutal demise.

The lore wasn't clear on what the blade would do to vampires. In Malcolm's case, it'd turned him into a vessel for Azerius. But then Dorian had killed the vessel, turning Malcolm's body to ash and banishing Azerius back to hell. They had no idea what, if anything, had happened to Malcolm's soul.

Through bleary eyes, Gabriel stared at the black blade, unable to form words. Unable to form a coherent thought.

For hundreds of years, the dagger had been hidden inside a sculpture—one Augustus had stolen from the former vampire king before he murdered him and usurped the throne.

Dorian and Charlotte had discovered it at Ravenswood a few months ago.

An expert in human art and antiquities, Charlotte had identified it as a Russian artifact known as the blade of the *Bessmertnym Soldat*—the Immortal Soldier—complete with a long and sordid history about all the human wars it'd helped win, all the human blood it'd spilled.

But eventually, they uncovered the truth of its origins— much older than the Russian tales. Much older than the entire span of human history.

The weapon Gabriel stared at now was the Blade of Azerius, forged by the demon himself in the bowels of hell.

Dorian had given it to Rogozin after the battle at Bloodbath as a downpayment for wiping out Chernikov's organization and aligning with House Redthorne. In addition to assassinating Chernikov, Rogozin had been prepared to pay Dorian ten million dollars for the thing.

Dorian had refused the money, using it to broker goodwill instead.

To say it was valuable to Rogozin was a gross understatement.

The fact that Rogozin had so easily left it behind—the fact that he'd even brought it with him tonight at all, well before he'd known the full extent of Viansa and Azerius' connection—could only mean one thing.

Alexei Rogozin, the formidable head of the most prominent demonic syndicate in the United States—arguably the most powerful demon on the earthly plane—was fucking terrified.

"We're going to need another plan," Gabriel said grimly. "And a hell of a lot more bourbon."

CHAPTER THIRTEEN

When Jaci was a child imprisoned in hell, she used to dream about spending Christmas in New York City.

Her father didn't celebrate the holiday itself, but he loved telling her about the lights, about the tourists ice-skating beneath the tree in Rockefeller Center, about how the entire city seemed to turn into a magical snow-globe village all at once. If you turned your head and squinted just a certain way, he'd said, you could almost believe it was all make-believe. Magic.

He'd painted such vivid pictures that Jaci almost felt like she'd grown up here too.

"We'll go one day," he'd said. "Soon as we get out of here, I'll take you to see the tree."

In the seven years she'd been in New York, Jaci still hadn't gone. She was never more than a subway ride away, but she just couldn't bring herself to go; as badly as she'd wanted to see it in person, the idea of visiting the tree without her father felt like giving up. Like she was accepting the fact that he'd never be able to take her himself.

Now, sitting alone in front of the fireplace in the Ravenswood study, watching a fresh snowfall gather on the windowsills outside, Jaci wondered whether her father even *remembered* Christmas. Remembered New York.

Remembered his daughter.

Tears stung the backs of her eyes, but she blinked them away and headed for the small bar, grateful Dorian hadn't run out of alcohol as quickly as he'd run out of blood.

"Gotta hand it to you royal vampires," she muttered, selecting a bottle of dark rum from the stash. "You sure know how to drink."

She poured a healthy shot into her mug of mint tea, then settled back into the soft leather chair in front of the fireplace, once again gazing out the frost-covered windows. Outside, the gardens of Ravenswood called to her—Charley had told her Dorian's roses bloomed year-round, and she'd hoped for a glimpse. But most of the blooms were covered in ice and snow, and it was much too cold tonight for an evening stroll anyway.

She needed Gabriel—missed him, even though it'd only been a few hours since she'd seen him. But she'd spent the entire afternoon and most of the evening poring over occult texts and playing magical mix-and-match with Isabelle, and with no obvious progress on their spells, she was barely clinging to hope.

One kiss from her vampire prince had the power to

chase the chill from her bones and the weariness from her heart, but Jaci wasn't sure when she'd get to see him tonight. He was currently locked in the dining room for the meeting with Alexei Rogozin. She had no idea what they hoped to accomplish in there, but Dorian seemed to think the demon could help them take down Viansa.

Worth a shot.

At this point, *anything* was worth a shot.

The fire popped, the snow blanketing the world beyond the windows, and Jaci tried to enjoy a few peaceful moments with her tea, grateful she even got them.

She exchanged a few texts with Maritza, who assured her Obsidian hadn't imploded in their absence, but Jaci demanded proof. Maritza sent a selfie—she and Enzo posing in front of the crowd at the bar, big smiles, half the vampires wearing goofy Santa hats. They'd even strung up some colored lights along the bar, totally breaking Gabriel's sleek aesthetic.

Don't you dare tell the boss! Maritza teased.

The scene sent a pang of longing through Jaci's chest.

She missed it, she realized. The city. The club. The bartending job. The life she'd been building here, the roots she'd never intended on planting somehow snaking into the ground without her permission, latching onto things she was still too afraid to admit she wanted.

Would she ever feel safe enough to call New York home?

To call *any* place home?

Jaci's throat tightened. More than anything, she wished

she could talk to her cousin. Meech had always had such a strong sense of place, of home. And her dimples and sass had never failed to shine a little light in the dark places of Jaci's heart.

But Jaci hadn't heard from Meech since before Viansa had crash-landed on the earthly plane, and now she was too terrified to even *attempt* another summoning. If Meech was off the grid—and Jaci truly hoped that was the case—better that she stay hidden. At least until Viansa was out of the picture.

"Mind if I hide in here with you?"

Jaci let out a little squeak and dropped her phone, but it was only Aiden, returning from a trip into town for some emergency blood bags from the clinic—just enough to hold them over until Dorian's regular delivery tomorrow.

"Not at all," she said with a smile. "I'd love some company."

"Likewise." He shut the door behind him and headed straight for the bar.

"Not in the mood to kiss Rogozin's ass tonight?" she teased. "The others are still in there."

"When it comes to snogging," he said, selecting a bottle of bourbon from the stash, "I'd rather go all in on the bottle than on Rogozin's puckered arse."

"Cheers to that." Jaci joined him at the bar and topped off her mug, the ratio of rum to tea tipping further into the rum direction.

"Where's Charlotte?" he asked. "I figured you two would be at least halfway to hammered by now, if not full-on blasted in the hot tub, giggling about some ridiculous film full of sparkly vampires."

"Sparkly vampire movie night is *next* week," Jaci teased. "Charley turned in early tonight. She spent most of the day helping me and Isabelle, but she was pretty wiped out. I made her go to bed an hour ago."

"Probably for the best," Aiden said as they settled in before the fire. "How's it going with Isabelle, anyway? Did the Spooky Sisters crack the case?"

"Still working on it. Isabelle will be back first thing tomorrow." Jaci sipped her boozy tea, trying to ignore the new chill that had taken up residence in her bones. "The problem is… We can draft a hundred versions of the spell, make a hundred potions to support it, write up a hundred predictions about the outcomes. But we can't test it on anyone but Viansa herself. And the moment we do, it's no longer a test—it either works, and we bind her, or it doesn't, and we die."

"Now *that's* the spirit," Aiden teased. Then, his voice turning as soft and kind as his eyes, "I know it's terrifying, Jacinda. Viansa, Azerius, the curse… It's a lot. But we're going to figure it out—I promise you. After all, we've got the world's foremost experts on the case."

"Experts?"

"Absolutely," he said with mock seriousness. "When it comes to dealing with toxic, dysfunctional families, the vampire royals are unparalleled. If anyone can devise a way to murder an evil half-sister and break the curse inspired by their terrible cunt of a father—forgive me, but it's the only word for him—it's the Redthornes."

Jaci couldn't help but laugh. Aiden just had that effect on people.

Reaching into his breast pocket, he retrieved a blood bag, then glanced at her. "Do you mind?"

"Not at all."

He tore off the top, then took a deep drink, alternating with sips of the bourbon, straight from the bottle.

"I'm not sure I could ever drink blood," she said. "All this time around vampires, and I still can't really wrap my head around it."

"It is a bit odd, isn't it? I've been a vampire for hundreds of years, and most days I can't wrap my head around it either. Today's emergency feeding frenzy notwithstanding, Charlotte still takes hers with gin." He took another sip from the bag. "When I was human, I couldn't stand the sight of blood. The smell. Even the word itself had the power to make me gag."

"How did you get used to it?"

"Dorian. After we were turned, there were times I wanted to… Well, not *die*, exactly. But give up. I hated being a vampire. Hated everything about it. Dorian though… He always made sure I ate. Found all sorts of ways to trick me into it. I swear the man was one step away from turning a spoonful of blood into an airplane and zooming it into my mouth."

Jaci cracked up. "Now *that* sounds like a fun story."

"Perhaps I'll share it at his wedding. I'm sure he'd love it."

"I can tell they mean a lot to you," she said softly. "It's sweet. I mean, even with all the teasing and bickering—the arguing—you're all so close. You say they're the experts on toxic families, but from where I'm sitting? Behind all those rough edges, all I see is love."

Something like regret flickered in Aiden's eyes, and he turned away from her, gazing into the fire and taking a deep drink from the bottle.

For a minute Jaci worried she'd said the wrong thing, but when he finally looked at her again, his eyes were full of warmth. Affection.

"Just a few months ago," he said softly, "Gabriel wouldn't have brought you here."

Jaci's cheeks flamed, her old insecurities rising to the surface. "Because he hates witches and demons, and I'm just—"

"No, love." Aiden reached out and touched her hand. "Because he wouldn't have shared something so important to him with me or his brothers. In fact, he wouldn't even speak to us at all."

"Oh. I… Right." Jaci lowered her eyes and nodded. Gabriel had shared a little about their past estrangement— other than Dorian and Aiden, who'd always been close, the rest of the brothers went fifty years without a single conversation. Then their father died, and the brothers returned home to deal with the aftermath.

In so many ways, they were still dealing with it. Probably always would be.

Jaci knew as well as anyone that some wounds never scarred over. You might get used to the pain—might go long stretches without feeling a thing, certain you were finally healed. But all it took was one cruel word, one cold glance, one dark memory clawing its way to the light, and suddenly you were on your knees again, desperately clutching your chest to keep your heart from falling out through the hole.

"The truth of it is, Jacinda," Aiden said, "you brought Gabriel back to us. And although he's a right pain in the arse on the *best* of days, all of us are grateful to even *have* those days with him again."

Jaci's eyes glazed with tears, and she nodded, unsure what to say.

A new smile dawned on Aiden's face, and he held up his glass in cheers. "Unfortunately for you, you're part of the family now, and there's no escaping. Welcome to the royal nuthouse—I hope you like to drink."

She touched the rim of her mug to his glass. "I *love* to drink."

"Excellent. Already fitting in."

"Speaking of new members of the family…" Jaci grinned and wriggled her eyebrows. "How are things going with Sasha?"

Aiden pressed a hand to his chest, gasping with mock indignation. "I'm certain I have no idea what you mean, Ms. Colburn."

"Whatever you say, Mr. Donovan." Jaci laughed, then sipped her tea. "She'll be here tomorrow, right?"

"We've got plans for sunrise coffee in Dorian's hot tub in the morning." He lowered his voice to a conspiratorial whisper. "I'm going to ask her to be my New Year's Eve date."

"Have you kissed her yet?"

Aiden turned the most adorable shade of red, then brought the bottle to his lips, totally dodging the question.

"Leave the poor vampire to his schoolgirl fantasies, Jacinda," a dark voice warned, and Jaci looked up to find Gabriel standing in the doorway, watching them.

"Gabriel," she breathed, the sight of him filling her with a mix of happiness and relief.

But *he* certainly didn't look relieved. Despite the amusement in his eyes, she couldn't help but notice the tick in his jaw, the tightness of his shoulder and arm muscles, the heaviness that seemed to follow him in like a storm cloud.

"You okay?" she asked, getting to her feet.

"Don't worry about your little princeling." Aiden laughed. "He's just jealous I didn't have to *kidnap* a woman to get her attention."

Gabriel glared at him. "Remind me again why I tolerate you?"

"Would you like the full report or just the highlights?"

"*Goodnight*, Aiden."

"Right." Aiden rose from his chair and headed for the door, stopping to pat Gabriel's cheek. "One day, Gabriel

Redthorne, you're going to wake up, and I'm not going to be here."

"Is that a promise?"

"You'll miss me terribly."

"I'd love the opportunity to do just that. Right now, as a matter of fact." Gabriel swiped the bottle of bourbon from Aiden's hand and jerked his head toward the door, his eyes still holding that spark of amusement. "Oh, look. I'm missing you already."

"But I haven't even left yet."

"*Goodnight*, Aiden bloody Donovan."

"*Goodnight*, princeling." Aiden grinned, then winked at Jaci. "See you at breakfast, love. I hear Dorian's cooking omelets."

"I want the full hot-tub coffee date report," she replied. "And no, not just the highlights."

"You got it."

Gabriel growled, and with a laugh that echoed down the hall, Aiden finally left them.

"Aiden is literally the sweetest vampire I've ever met, which is saying a lot." Jaci slid her hands over Gabriel's shoulders and smiled. "I mean, you guys act like these big, brooding, scary monsters, but when it comes down to it, you're all a bunch of softies."

"Softies. Right." Hands finding their way to her hips, Gabriel kicked the door shut behind him and leaned back against it, pulling her closer.

"He and Sasha are so cute together," she said. "Don't you think?"

Gabriel kissed her jaw. "Bloody adorable."

"How cool is it that Charley's sister is with Dorian's best friend? I mean, what are the chances?"

"No idea." He dragged his mouth to her ear, inhaling deeply, his hands sliding over her ass.

"Where did Dorian learn how to cook?" she asked. "How come you don't cook?"

"I pay people to cook."

"How'd it go with Rogozin? Did you guys figure out how to take out Viansa?"

"We may have a weapon," he said, blazing a trail of hot kisses down the side of her neck.

"What kind of weapon?"

"I'll tell you all about it tomorrow." Gabriel brought his mouth back to hers, hovering close, his breath warm.

"But I—"

"Jacinda?"

"Yes?"

He arched that devastatingly sexy eyebrow, his green eyes sparkling. "I don't want to talk about Rogozin and his weapons. Or sweet, adorable Aiden. I don't want to talk about Dorian's cooking or Cole's sexy battle scars or Colin's Disney-prince hair or any of the many, many reprobates who line up behind the bar at Obsidian every night just to catch a glimpse at the infamous Jacinda Colburn."

Jaci slid her fingers into his hair, her body pressed tight against his. Through a grin, she said, "Jealous, Prince?"

He huffed out a laugh. "Absolutely not. I mean, mostly not. Yes. *Maybe*."

"Maybe?" She brought her mouth to his throat, kissing and nipping the skin, making him shudder.

"Devil's *balls*, woman. Everything about you drives me wild. I could scarcely keep my wits about me in that meeting. All I could think about was hunting you down and…" He pulled her closer, his cock hard and insistent against her belly.

"Hmm. Does this mean I'm being punished again?"

"Now *that* is a question I'm happy to answer." He reached behind him and locked the study door, a wicked grin gracing that sexy, filthy mouth. "You are *definitely* being punished. And I'm not letting up until I make you *scream*."

CHAPTER FOURTEEN

A shiver rolled through Jaci's body, her thighs clenching as Gabriel lowered his wicked mouth to hers, brushing her lips with a kiss as soft as a breeze.

"Close your eyes, witch," he whispered. "Don't open them until I command it."

She did as he asked, her body buzzing with anticipation as his breath ghosted across her mouth, his evergreens-in-winter scent surrounding her.

With a delicate touch that made her *insanely* wet, Gabriel unbuttoned her shirt, one button at a time. Pushing it off her shoulders, he lowered his mouth to the top of her breasts, dragging his tongue from one curve to the other, his thumbs scraping over her nipples, teasing her through the lace bra.

"Gabriel," she breathed. Melted.

Holy hell, the things this man can do with his mouth…

"You're not talking tonight, moonflower," he said. *"I'm*

talking. About all the things I'm going to do to you, one breath, one touch, one kiss at a time."

He shifted back to her mouth again and bit her lower lip, tugging gently.

Jaci sighed, wanting nothing more than to follow the force of that tug and fall right into him.

His hands trailed up her back and unclasped her bra, sliding it off her shoulders and dropping it to the floor.

With her eyes closed, Jaci's other senses were on high alert, Gabriel's every touch leaving a trail of fire in its wake.

"First, I'm going to finish stripping you bare," he said, and she held her breath, heart thundering as she awaited the next sensation.

It came along her abdomen, soft fingers sliding across her skin, dipping inside the waistband of her jeans, slowly pushing the button through the hole. He tugged down the zipper, slid the fabric down over her hips.

A rush of cool air swirled around her as the infuriating vampire dropped to his knees, slowly guiding her out of the last scraps of clothing.

Jaci stood bare, her back to the fireplace, the warmth of the flames on her backside a stark contrast to the cool air caressing her nipples. For a long beat, she heard nothing but the crackling fire, felt nothing but the absence of Gabriel's touch.

She opened her mouth to speak, the desperate need to obey his commands warring with an even more desperate need to call him back. Everything in her fucking *burned* for him. If he didn't fuck her soon—with his hands, his mouth, his mouthwatering cock—the wait alone would surely incinerate her.

"Gabriel," she finally blurted out. "Where are you?"

"Tsk, tsk, little moonflower," he whispered. Somehow, he was behind her now, his hot mouth close to her ear. "I told you, no talking. Now I'll have to add another punishment to the long, long list of things I'm going to do to you."

The air around her shifted again, and then he was in front once more, fingers sliding up her neck and into her hair, pulling it until she tilted her head back, giving him unrestricted access to her throat. The tip of his nose tracing a path from her jaw to her collarbone, then back up again.

His every touch sizzled, sending tiny spasms of pleasure reverberating through her core, straight up her spine.

She wanted him to bite her again. To sink his fangs into the spot just beneath her ear, his tongue working over her flesh as he drank from her, slowly losing control…

"You need to come," he murmured, his voice as jagged as his breathing. "The scent of your desire is… overpowering."

"Hmm. Who's fault is that?"

The insubordination earned her a smack on the ass that did nothing to cool the surge of heat between her thighs.

"Naughty little witch." Gabriel slid his fingers out of her hair, slowly trailing down to her breasts, her nipples, her stomach. His wandering hands finally settled on her hips, and with a firm grip, he tugged her forward.

"Three steps," he said softly, guiding her in the direction of one of the chairs. "That's it. Right here."

She felt him sit down, then he pulled her into his lap.

Keeping her eyes shut tight, she straddled him, shocked to feel he was naked too.

She hadn't even heard him undress, but now he sat beneath her, his rock-hard body hot and slick where their skin touched—his hands on her ass, her knees bracketing his hips.

Gabriel leaned forward, his mouth close to hers once more. "Open your legs for me."

She obeyed, parting her thighs as much as she could in the chair and shifting forward until she felt the hot press of his cock at her entrance.

"I've been dreaming of this moment all night," he said softly. "Making you come on my cock. Hearing you *beg* me for it."

A whimper escaped her lips.

"It's what you want too, is it not?" he asked. "My cock sliding between your thighs, fucking you until you break for me?"

"It's *all* I want," she admitted, no longer able to hold back. "Please, Gabriel. Don't make me wait—"

He gripped her ass and slid inside her, cutting her off with a deep thrust so perfect, so intense it brought tears to her eyes.

"Show me," he said, guiding her hips into a slow roll. "Show me just how you want me to punish you."

She rose up on her knees, then slid down his shaft, every inch of him filling her all over again. He rocked forward to meet her, then pulled back, their bodies sliding apart, then joining once more. Every movement was slow and perfect, an erotic dance that set her nerves ablaze and made her delirious with pleasure, but it wasn't enough.

Gabriel had tormented her with this game for too long, and now, her body was all out of patience. *She* was all out of patience.

She increased the pace, taking him in deeper, and Gabriel followed her lead, sliding his hands around to cup her ass, pulling her close as he sucked one nipple, then the other, his stubbled jaw scratching her skin, heat building between her thighs.

She rode him harder, faster, wanting only to get closer, to feel him deep inside, filling her, stretching her, pushing her closer to that blissful edge…

"*Jacinda*," he ground out, hands gripping her hips, forcing her to slow her frantic thrusts.

She finally opened her eyes. Deprived of her vision earlier, it took Jaci a minute to adjust, a blur of colors and shapes slowly sharpening into focus.

"You just couldn't wait, could you." Gabriel grinned up at her, his eyes golden in the firelight as he brushed the hair away from her face. "For that, I'm revoking your topping privileges. Back on the bottom you go."

"What?" Jaci laughed. "This was all a ploy. You totally set me up to fail just so you could be on top again."

"Guilty as charged." He flashed that maddening smirk, then wrapped his arms around her and rose from the chair, still holding her close.

A fleece blanket hung over the back of the other chair,

and he grabbed it with one hand and tossed it onto the floor in front of the fireplace. Wordlessly he knelt down and laid Jaci on her back, then leaned forward, his mouth descending on her throat. He kissed down to her collarbone, then back up, nuzzling her neck, feathering along her jaw, then slowly working his way back down.

Jaci fisted his hair, tugging him to bring him back to her mouth, but Gabriel shook his head, the rumble of his laughter making her stomach fizz.

"I'm in charge now," he teased, running his firm hands up her inner thighs, slowly pushing them apart. "All you need to do is lie back and take your punishment."

"Punishment. Right. You *really* need a new dic—"

"A new dick? Surely the warranty on the original hasn't expired yet." Still grinning, he lowered his dark head between her thighs.

The ghost of a sigh.

A deep, sensual growl.

The flick of a hot tongue teasing her clit.

"Dictionary!" she cried out, tightening her grip on his hair. "Holy fucking *shit*, you're… I can't even… Is that… Oh, fuck. *Gabriel*…"

A whole bunch of other nonsense fell out of her mouth, but Jaci had no idea what language she was speaking now, and her vampire prince wasn't listening anyway. He was already gone, lost in the rhythmic thrusts of his tongue, the hot caress of his mouth on her flesh.

The things he was doing to her… *Damn*. Maybe Jaci needed a new dictionary too, because when she tried to find the words to describe the event of Gabriel Redthorne unleashing his special brand of hell between her thighs, she couldn't think of a single one.

With every delicious stroke, he chased the thoughts from her head, the worries from her heart, the fear, all of it. He kissed her until she forgot where she was. He kissed her until she was weak and dizzy. He kissed her until her mind evaporated and she was nothing but a collection of sighs and sensations, vibrating and pulsing, liquifying beneath the command of his filthy, insatiable mouth.

Then, sucking her clit between his lips, he thrust two fingers inside her, curving them just right.

"Tell me to stop," he growled.

"Don't stop."

"Are you certain?" He thrust in harder, bringing his mouth back to her clit, circling it with his tongue as he stroked her with his fingers, deeper, faster…

"Gabriel!" She came with a sharp gasp, her muscles seizing, then releasing, melting into nothingness once more as the orgasm rocketed through her entire body, wave after wave after wave.

Her legs were still quaking when Gabriel gripped her thighs again, hauled her close, and collapsed on top of her, spearing her with a single, perfect thrust that had her chasing another orgasm, her body clenching hard around him.

She raked her nails down his back and clutched his firm ass, driving him deeper inside, still begging him not to stop. Not now. Not ever.

Another growl rumbled through his chest, dark and possessive and so fucking sexy it made her heart stutter, and he claimed her mouth in a suffocating kiss and speared her one last time, his body shuddering against her as they fell headlong together into that euphoric, fiery abyss.

The fire had died down to embers, Jaci and Gabriel lying naked on their backs, an icy wind lashing the windows outside, but Jaci wasn't cold.

After everything her vampire had just done to her, she was pretty sure she'd never be cold again.

She rolled onto her hip and snuggled closer, but this time when Gabriel wrapped her in his arms, something felt off.

Is he… trembling?

"Gabriel?"

"Hmm?" His eyes were closed, his breathing deep and untroubled, but Jaci couldn't shake the feeling that something was wrong.

"Are you feeling okay?" she asked.

No response.

She slid a hand across his chest. His skin felt cool. Clammy. "What's going on?"

He grabbed her hand, pressed a kiss to her palm. Let out a deep sigh.

But he still didn't answer her.

"Look at me," she said urgently, and after an impossibly

long moment, he finally obeyed, opening his eyes and capturing her gaze.

And there, darkening the eyes of the man she loved— the *vampire* she loved—was a look of fear so intense, so desperate, it nearly swallowed her whole.

"What's happening?" she whispered.

"It's nothing to worry about." He turned his head away from her and stared up at the ceiling. "I'm just a bit tired. Long day."

"You don't get tired. Not like this." She cupped his face. "Talk to me."

With a resigned sigh, he rolled onto his hip and faced her, his mouth drawn into a tight frown. He reached up and tucked a lock of hair behind her ear, then closed his eyes, turning his arm over to reveal the underside.

He clenched his fist, the veins darkening beneath his skin.

Isabelle's magical tattoos were no longer visible.

Jaci ran her finger from his wrist to his elbow. "But… they're just… gone?"

Gabriel nodded and opened his eyes. "Isabelle's doing her best, but now they're fading almost as soon as she makes them."

"But… why?"

"The curse has one job, Jacinda," he said softly. "And it's going to do that job by any means necessary. If it can't poison our blood directly, it'll interfere with the magic that helps us survive."

"You need to feed."

He nodded. "Tomorrow. Dorian's got a delivery coming."

"Aiden made a run to the clinic earlier. There's some in the kitchen." She tried to get up, but Gabriel grabbed her hand, tugging her back down.

"It's gone, Jace. Dorian… He was in bad shape after the meeting. I told him to finish it off."

Jaci took a deep breath, trying not to freak out. More blood was on the way. The Redthornes were in rough shape, but this wasn't insurmountable. Not yet.

But until Viansa was out of the picture—permanently—this would always be a race against time.

Without another thought, she lifted her hand and pressed her wrist to his mouth. "Bite."

Gabriel let out a soft laugh. "Are you trying to kill me?"

"The poison we used on Renault is already out of my system."

"Jacinda, I just fed from you the other night. And after all the magic you expended at the warehouse, not to mention the stress of dealing with Viansa… No. You need to recover—"

"Recover?" She glared at him, letting her eyes turn black. "Feed, Prince. Or I'll light you up and *re-cover* this room with your ashes."

"Tough words from such a little witch," he muttered beneath the insistent press of her wrist. "I should punish you all over again."

"Yes, you *totally* should. But later. Right now, you've got *one* job." She shot him another demon death-glare. "Stop talking and start sucking, vampire."

"Sucking. Right." He cupped her breast, dragging a thumb across her nipple. "I do like the sound of that."

"The blood, dickhead."

"Fine." He let out a put-upon sigh, then took the offered wrist between his fingers, rubbing it lightly to stimulate the vein. "But only because you're so adorable when you boss me around. Even more adorable than your precious Aiden."

"Now *that's* high praise."

Gabriel laughed and tried to act like he was merely indulging her, and she laughed and let him think he was getting away with it.

But when his fangs finally descended and pierced her skin, not even the deeply erotic thrill of his bite could chase away the worry churning through her insides.

Gabriel and his family were getting weaker.

The curse was getting stronger.

And time, as it so often did, was about to kick *all* their asses.

Wake up, lab rat…

Jaci's mind skimmed along the border between asleep and awake. She thought she'd been dreaming, but something tugged at her subconscious…

Lab rat…

A dark whisper against the back of her neck. A prickle of unease skittering down her spine.

That's right, lab rat. Your sister's back…

"Hmm?" she murmured.

Was she still dreaming? Where was she?

Was someone calling her? The voice sounded so familiar. So close…

I've got a surprise for you, lab rat…

Jaci gasped, a bolt of fear burning away the cobwebs in her mind. Her eyes flew open, confirming the worst.

Viansa loomed over her, glossy red lips stretched into an evil grin.

"I told you, lab rat," she taunted. "You took *my* vampire. Now I'm taking yours."

"No!" Jaci bolted upright, and the gruesome image vanished.

"Jace?" Gabriel sat up next to her, holding her close. Tight.

"I thought she took you," Jaci whispered. Her frantic heartbeat thudded in her ears, the rush of blood making her dizzy.

"It's okay, love," he said. "No one took me. I'm right here."

Jaci blew out a breath. Gabriel's warm embrace grounded her.

The darkness faded away.

The study. She was on the couch in the study. She and Gabriel had fallen asleep there after he'd fed. Hours ago, from the looks of it.

The sun hadn't yet risen; orange and purple streaked the indigo sky. It was no longer snowing. No longer windy.

She glanced down at her wrist. The puncture wounds had already healed, leaving nothing but a dull ache to remind her of the bite.

Alive. She was alive. Gabriel was alive.

It was just a nightmare. Just her succubus asshole sister trying to get inside her head and scramble it all up.

"Okay?" Gabriel asked, pressing a kiss to her forehead, and she nodded, the now-familiar brush of his lips calming her.

"Just a nightmare," she whispered, desperate to believe it.

And for a minute, she almost did.

Then an ear-splitting, blood-curdling scream shattered the pre-dawn peace, and Jaci knew—in a terrifying instant —it hadn't been a nightmare at all.

CHAPTER FIFTEEN

Gabriel and Jacinda reached the backyard just seconds after Dorian and Charlotte, all of them hastily dressed, still blinking sleep from their eyes, shocked into utter paralysis by the sight.

In the frozen, predawn darkness, a young woman stood at the end of Dorian's infinity pool, bundled in winter gear, waist-deep in the water. Her breath misted in white clouds, her body trembling so violently it sent ripples out across the surface of the water.

Gabriel sucked in an icy breath. Blinked. Tried to make sense of a thing that defied all logic.

Is that… Sasha?

He blinked again. It was definitely Sasha.

And there, floating face-down in front of the girl, looking as dead as any man Gabriel had ever seen in such a state, was Aiden Donovan.

"Aiden?" Gabriel whispered, the impossibility of the whole scene making his thoughts slow and fuzzy, as if his mind were wading through molasses.

"That's... That's my sister." Charlotte's voice was equally soft, equally confused.

Next to Gabriel, Jacinda shivered but said nothing.

Even Dorian was immobilized.

"But it's… nearly Christmas," he said, as if that had anything to do with it. "It's too dark for swimming."

All of this unfolded in a matter of seconds.

Heartbeats.

Then the girl touched Aiden's body and screamed again.

"Brimstone," Jacinda said suddenly, then gasped, the sound of it finally shattering the shock-induced trance.

Awareness slammed into Gabriel at once.

"Are you certain?" he asked.

"Viansa was here," she said, her voice tight with panic. "It wasn't a nightmare, Gabriel. She was *here*. She warned me she was going to take him. She said we killed her vampire, so she—"

"Jacinda, listen to me." Gabriel grabbed her shoulders, needing to steady himself with the touch as badly as he needed to steady her. "Go back inside and run two warm baths—not too hot. Put on the kettle as well. We'll need to warm them up slowly. And call Isabelle. Tell her what's happened."

"But Aiden—"

"Can you do that for me? Please?"

Jacinda blinked up at him, the last of the confusion and panic finally clearing from her eyes.

"Two warm baths," she said firmly. "Kettle. Isabelle. I'm on it."

Jacinda dashed back into the manor, and the three vampires blurred to the pool and jumped in. The water itself was heated, but the air was not, quickly sucking the warmth from their upper bodies. All of them gasped and shivered, the curse doing its damndest to drain the last of their remaining energy.

"Sasha," Charlotte said, her teeth chattering as she reached for her sister's arm. "You need to get out of the water, baby. Come on. Come with me."

"Don't touch me!" Sasha recoiled from Charlotte's touch as if it'd scorched her. "Don't you fucking touch me!"

"It's okay." Charlotte raised her hands in surrender and lowered her voice. "I just want to help. Will you let me help you?"

"Help?" Sasha gaped at her as if she'd never seen the woman before.

Dorian shot Gabriel a worried glance.

"It's dangerous out here in the cold," Charlotte explained, slowly trying to shift the girl's attention away from Aiden. "Our bodies are losing heat too quickly. We should go inside and sit by the fire. Have some hot chocolate. Doesn't that sound nice?"

With Sasha's gaze temporarily locked on Charlotte, Dorian and Gabriel moved to Aiden, slowly turning him over. He was stiff and cold to the touch, eyes wide open and glassy. Unblinking. Unmoving.

Everything about him was deadly still.

"He's dead," Sasha whispered, pushing past Charlotte in the water. She placed her hand on Aiden's chest, her mouth parted in a silent cry of agony that tore right through Gabriel's heart.

"He's not dead," Dorian said softly, though he didn't sound all that convinced. "Can you tell us what happened?"

"I... I..." Sasha blinked, looking up at Dorian with wide, terrified eyes.

"It's all right, love," he said. "Tell me what happened."

"We were supposed to have coffee in the hot tub and watch the sunrise," Sasha said. "But how can he watch the sunrise if he's dead? Dead people can't see. Right?"

Fuck. She was going into shock. If they didn't get her out of there soon, she'd be hypothermic.

They'd *all* be hypothermic.

"I took a cab from my apartment," she said. "I wanted to beat traffic—I was worried I'd be late and miss it."

"The date?" Dorian asked.

"The sunrise."

Dorian offered a sympathetic smile.

"But after the driver dropped me off, I realized I didn't have a key. And I didn't want to wake anyone inside, so I just came around back."

While Sasha was occupied with Dorian and Charlotte, Gabriel moved Aiden's body to the edge of the pool, trying to find his pulse. A heartbeat. Any signs of life at all.

But everywhere he touched, there was only ice. Only death.

One day, Gabriel Redthorne, you're going to wake up, and I'm not going to be here...

A wave of fear slammed into Gabriel's chest, stealing his breath. His heart hammered so hard he swore it would shatter his ribs.

You'll miss me terribly...

Aiden wasn't dead. He couldn't be dead. He was still here. Present. Solid.

Dead vampires weren't solid. They were ash.

Dead vampires were *fucking* ash.

He repeated the words like a mantra as he hopped up onto the heated wooden deck that surrounded the back edge of the pool and pulled Aiden out, desperately trying to rub some warmth back into the man's ice-cold hands.

He was fully dressed, just like Sasha. Coat. Boots. All of it.

Dead vampires are ash... Dead vampires are ash...

"When I got here," Sasha continued, "I realized I forgot the coffee. I'd told Aiden I'd have the driver run me into town on the way up—I wanted to pick up some donuts too. The powdered sugar kind?"

Dorian nodded. "Aiden loves those."

"Yeah, but I totally spaced it. I pulled out my phone, thinking I could order delivery or something, but then I saw him."

"Aiden?" Charlotte asked.

"He was coming from the direction of the guest house. I called out for him, and he looked up, and we saw each other and we both smiled and I forgot about the coffee and the stupid donuts because it was just this... I don't know. This perfect moment, you know?"

Dorian forced another smile, but Gabriel's heart cracked in half, the fucking girl and her fucking story and everything about this fucking scene making him ache with a loss he simply *refused* to acknowledge. It was ridiculous to even consider it. There *was* no loss, no reason to ache, because there was no *fucking* way any of this was actually happening, and as soon as Aiden stopped fucking around and admitted this was nothing but a twisted prank, Gabriel was going to kick his wet vampire arse from here to hell and back again.

"What happened next?" Dorian asked.

"Then he just... I don't know. He gave me this really weird look like he didn't even recognize me anymore. And I started walking toward him, but he just..." She sucked in a breath, her voice breaking. "He fell face-first into the pool. And he never came back up."

Dead vampires, Gabriel reminded himself. *Ash.*

He pressed an ear to Aiden's chest.

No heartbeat. No rise and fall of breath. Nothing.

"I jumped in and when I touched him his skin was so cold. Like, ice-cold, which made no sense. He wasn't in the water that long, and the water's warm, and... Oh, God."

She looked over at Aiden and Gabriel on the deck, and her face crumpled. "He's dead, isn't he?"

The quiet agony in her voice worse than her violent screams. Worse than any sound Gabriel had ever heard in his life.

"He's not dead, love," Dorian said. "Vampires can't drown."

"Then it's hypothermia or a head injury or a heart attack or poison or—"

"We can't freeze," he continued. "We don't have heart attacks. And when we die—no matter how it happens—we turn to ash."

"Ash," Gabriel repeated, needing to taste the word in his mouth. To feel the shape of it. To remind himself the rules of nature still applied, even to immortals, even in the face of an original demon.

Logic.

Reason.

Rules.

Aiden couldn't *possibly* be dead.

"Always?" Sasha asked, and she and Gabriel both looked to Dorian for the answer.

In that moment, Gabriel couldn't recall a time when he'd felt so young. So lost. So in need of his brother's guidance.

Dorian was the eldest Redthorne. The fucking *vampire* king.

If he said a thing, it *had* to be true.

Didn't it?

"Always," Dorian said, and Gabriel nearly wept to hear it.

Always.

"I'd offer to demonstrate," Dorian continued, "but I doubt Gabriel will let me stake him."

"Maybe after the new year," Gabriel managed, and—a fucking Christmas miracle—the girl finally smiled.

In her brief time on the periphery of Gabriel's life, Sasha had annoyed him, vexed him, angered him, teased him, irritated him, and—on one or two occasions—ever-so-slightly amused him.

But suddenly, somehow, that smile was his lifeline.

It was everything. The hope he desperately needed. The sunrise on a frigid winter morn.

"Why don't you get out of the water, love," Dorian said gently. "Go inside with your sister. Gabriel and I will take good care of Aiden."

With a string of promises from Dorian and Gabriel both, Sasha finally allowed Charlotte to lead her out of the pool and inside the house.

Dorian joined Gabriel on the deck with Aiden, and Jacinda was back too, crouching down beside them, her eyes full of concern.

"The baths are ready," she said. "Isabelle's on her way."

Gabriel tried to smile, but couldn't. His hand was on Aiden's chest, desperate to feel a heart that just kept refusing to beat.

"How is he?" Jacinda brushed the wet hair back from Aiden's forehead.

Gabriel shook his head, but then…

Wait. Was that…

"Bloody hell," he said. "Do that again."

Jacinda ran her fingers through Aiden's hair, and sure enough, it happened again. A slight fluttering against Aiden's palm. A beat. Then another. Stronger. Louder.

"His heartbeat," Gabriel said. "It's faint. Too slow. But it's there, getting stronger with every second. He's breathing again too. Fucking hell, he's breathing."

Emotion tightened his throat, making his eyes water.

Fucking hell, he was going to kick Aiden's ass for that too.

"Get him inside," Dorian said. "I'll phone Colin. Maybe it's some kind of coma—"

"Colin will know what to do," Gabriel said, clinging to that hope, to the memory of Sasha's smile, to the warmth of the sun that'd just begun its morning ascent. He lifted Aiden into his arms and got to his feet, ignoring the exhaustion in his limbs, the ache in his fingers, the bite of winter on wet skin. "Between Colin and Isabelle, they'll figure out how to bring him out of the coma and—"

"Oh, shit," Jacinda whispered, her brow tightening with some new worry. "No. This can't be happening. Not again. Not like this."

Gabriel's heart dropped into his stomach. "Jace?"

She finally met his gaze, the raw fear in her eyes shattering Gabriel's hope. She shook her head, unable to voice it, and in that terrible instant—in that terrible silence—he knew. He fucking *knew*.

Jacinda had seen this before. Had watched it happen to her father seven years ago, just minutes after he'd finally delivered his daughter to New York. To freedom.

Aiden Donovan wasn't in a coma.

He was in hell.

CHAPTER SIXTEEN

There was no more time for flipping through lore books and mixing batches of potions. No time for spellcraft. No time for gathering allies and working through scenarios and drawing up plans A, B, or even C.

Viansa had dragged Aiden's soul to hell, imprisoning him just as she'd imprisoned Zachary Colburn.

And there was only one thing to be done about it.

Unfortunately, the demanding, infuriating, uptight vampire king insisted on overcomplicating matters.

As usual.

"I can't believe I'm about to say this," Gabriel said, "but no, brother. For once in your immortal life, I *don't* want you to go to hell."

"Not my first choice for a holiday either, but it's Christmas Eve, Gabriel. All the best places are booked." Dorian slid the Blade of Azerius into its sheath and strapped it to his chest. "You'll find a copy of my will and a

165

few other legal documents in a safe at the north end of the crypts. It's biometrically keyed to your blood, so to open it, you—"

"It has to be me."

"You just press your finger to the scanner, and—"

"You know I'm right. Jacinda's got the lay of the land, and together she and I can—"

"You'll feel a little prick, then—"

"Listen to me, Dorian."

"When you hear the beep, you'll know it's—"

"*Dorian!*"

The man finally shut his mouth. Blew out a long, slow breath. When he spoke again, his voice was maddeningly calm. "We've gone over this a hundred times, Gabriel. Aiden needs me. I won't abandon him to Viansa or any other of hell's tormentors."

"Nor will I. And Aiden's not the only soul in need of rescue. We go down there, we've got one shot. *One.* If we don't find Zachary—"

"I'm well aware of the mission. You don't need to repeat it."

Gabriel shoved a hand through his hair, damn near ready to tear it out. "Be reasonable, for once in your life. You can't go. You simply can't. I'm—"

"Not the king." Dorian turned his attention back to the strap around his chest. "This is my duty, not yours."

"Your duty, *king,* is to protect your family and your people here. In *our* realm. For fuck's sake, Dorian. Azerius has been salivating for the taste of your charred balls ever since you banished him, and you think you can just waltz down into his domain, take out the succubus working to set him free, grab two souls, and slip away undetected? Oh, that's assuming you can even find the souls, which you bloody well can't because you don't know where the fuck you're going! Honestly, brother. Please tell me you're not that daft."

"And you think *you've* got a better chance?"

The frustration that'd been simmering in Gabriel's gut kicked up to a full-on boil.

Enough was enough.

"Give me the blade," he demanded. "*Now*."

"Or what?" Dorian finally met his gaze again, spearing Gabriel with a deadly glare. "Last I checked, *Prince,* there was only one vampire king."

"Drag yourself to hell, *highness*, and how many vampire kings will we have then?"

Dorian folded his arms across his chest. Kept right on glaring.

"Give you a hint," Gabriel said. "Starts with a Z. Rhymes with hero."

No response from the impenetrable vampire king.

"Not even a guess?" Gabriel pressed.

"Fuck off, Gabriel. I outrank you. End of discussion."

"Outrank me?"

"If you've got a problem with it, take it up with Father."

"*You* take it up with Father. You're about five minutes from joining him in the eternal fire, practically ready to run into his arms."

"I'll let him know you asked after him." Dorian checked the strap once more, then headed for the door, knocking into Gabriel's shoulder as he passed.

But Gabriel wasn't about to let him leave. Not like this. Not at all.

He rushed at Dorian in a blur. Slammed him into the wall so hard he cracked the plaster. And then, with a surge of rage and terror and love and brotherhood and the last-ditch effort of a truly desperate, incredibly stupid vampire, he punched a hole through his brother's chest and wrapped his fingers around that still-beating, infamously tender heart.

Dorian's eyes widened in shock, his jaw clenched tight against the sudden pain.

"You're not... going to... kill me," he panted. "So enough with the... theatrics."

Gabriel let him sit with it. Just for a moment. Just long enough to make the point.

Then he shrugged and said, "You're right. I'm not going to kill you. Not today, at least." He released the heart and drew back, slowly easing out his hand. As quickly as he'd made the hole, it healed. "I just wanted you to know that I could. That quickly, Dorian. Half a second. Azerius won't grant you the same courtesy."

For the span of several heartbeats, Dorian said nothing. Did nothing. And Gabriel stood like a statue before him, watching as the fury rose in his eyes, gathered in his muscles, swirled around him like the coming storm.

"*Move!*" Dorian roared.

Gabriel refused to budge. "If you won't listen to reason, and you won't listen to my bloody fist in your chest, you listen to this." He leaned in close. Whispered the one word that held the power to break through Dorian's stubborn rage. "*Charlotte.*"

A dark, fiery red chased away the golden-brown of Dorian's irises, his fangs descending, a growl rumbling through his chest. "I don't know what game you're playing," he ground out, "but so help me, Gabriel—"

"Charlotte D'Amico," Gabriel said. "Your fiancée. Soon to be your queen. *Our* queen. Presently upstairs trying to sedate her sister, a girl who's bloody traumatized after finding the vampire she's in love with floating in your infinity pool bereft of a soul."

"I am *warning* you—"

"No, you fucking twat. I'm warning *you.*" Gabriel jabbed a finger at Dorian's chest, damn near trembling with the force of his wrath. "The minute Charlotte comes downstairs and realizes you walked through that hell portal, there's no *way* she's not following. Straight into the lair of the very demon who once had a claim on her soul—a claim you destroyed when you defeated him at Bloodbath. I'm sure Azerius would just *love* to welcome her into his bed, especially after he makes her a widow by incinerating the fucking vampire king. So if you won't sit this one out for me, for Colin, for Cole, for Aiden himself—who, by the way, would kick your arse if he knew what you were up to —then for fuck's sake, Dorian. Do it for her. You fucking do this for *her.*"

For an eternity, no one said another word. No one moved. No one blinked.

And then, finally, a tiny crack appeared in the rock-hard facade, and Dorian closed his eyes and lowered his head, the breath rushing from his lungs in a long, defeated sigh.

"You asked me to trust you on Rogozin," Gabriel said softly, the last of his anger abating as the weight of what lay ahead fully settled on them both, "and I have. Now I need you to trust *me* on this. This *one* thing." He closed his eyes, every one of his old regrets rushing to the surface, jabbing at the softest parts of his heart. "I know, Dorian. I *know* I've made mistakes. I've been foolish, reckless, violent, down right suicidal at times, and if I could change the past—"

"The past is dead," Dorian whispered.

"But the present isn't. This *family* isn't. And I swear to you, brother, I will do whatever I have to do to protect what's left of it. What's left of us. I just need you to give me the chance."

Dorian lifted his head. A tear tracked down his stern face. "I bloody hate this," he said softly, but he was already removing the strap from his chest, fastening it around Gabriel's and pulling it tight.

"I *will* bring him back to you," Gabriel said. "I swear it."

"I know you will. I…" Dorian closed his eyes, his voice a broken whisper. "Gabriel…"

But whatever he'd meant to say, the words never came.

After another beat, Gabriel turned away, and they retreated to opposite sides of the study, Dorian at the desk in the corner, Gabriel at the bar.

Dorian cleared his throat. When he spoke again, his voice was clear and firm. Kingly. "Best be off, then. Our enemies won't vanquish themselves."

Gabriel laughed, then selected the most expensive bottle of bourbon from the collection and tossed it at Dorian, who caught it easily.

"Keep the drinks ready and the fire stoked," he said. "We'll be back before the bourbon warms and the embers cool."

Dorian glanced up at him, a smile curving his lips. "See to it that you are."

.

CHAPTER SEVENTEEN

For the first time in seven years, Jaci was going home.

Not to introduce the man she loved to her family, or to show him around her old stomping grounds, or to cruise the streets and marvel at how much the place had changed since the good ol' days.

No, Jaci was going home to rescue the imprisoned souls of her father and her friend.

To hunt down and kill her sister.

To break the curse that would otherwise doom the Redthorne vampires—vampires that had become her family —to certain death.

And, last but definitely not least, to stop an ancient demon from manifesting in his true form and turning the entire planet into his personal torture chamber.

But, you know. No pressure or anything.

"Are you all right?" Gabriel slid a hand behind her neck, gently stroking her with his thumb.

"Not in the slightest. You?"

"Never been worse, honestly." He laughed and planted a kiss on her cheek. "But on the bright side, I do love to travel. See new places. Take in the local culture."

"In that case, I'll do my best to be a good tour guide. But you better tip well, Prince, or I'm only taking you to the tourist traps."

"You've got yourself a deal, demon." His eyes sparkled with mischief, but the light faded quickly, the reality settling in hard and fast.

They were down in the crypts, watching as Isabelle made the final preparations for their hell portal. Charley was still upstairs with Sasha, but Aiden was stretched out on the stone floor behind Isabelle, still unconscious, but breathing. Dorian and Cole were keeping a close eye on him.

Colin, who'd spent the night at the hospital trying but failing to save the young victim of the mage sacrifice, was now on his way back to Ravenswood in a helicopter, a new patient entrusted into his care.

Zachary Colburn.

Soon, her father's body would be lying next to Aiden's, both awaiting the return of their souls.

"Almost there," Isabelle said.

Spread out on the stone floor in front of her, five black candles flickered to life, one at each point on a pentagram. The symbol itself had been painted with a mix of Jaci's and Gabriel's blood, the whole thing surrounded by a circle of salt and protective crystals—obsidian, black tourmaline, black kyanite. It was supposed to keep them safe during the departure and ensure they didn't bring back any unwanted guests on the return.

"So how does this work, exactly?" Gabriel asked.

"Physical beings who travel to hell need a portal," Isabelle said. "Absent a demonic summoning ritual, we have to create one. Essentially, we're opening the same sort of channel we would in a summoning, but not inviting anyone in."

"Hopefully," Jaci added. "That's why we've got the crystals."

"Once you get there," Isabelle said, "you'll need to move quickly. Your personal connections to Aiden and Zachary should help guide you to the location of their souls —they'll be drawn to you, just like you'll be drawn to them —but you've also got Viansa working against you, and possibly other demons."

"Actually," Jaci said, "there's a good chance Viansa *wants* us to find them this time. She took Aiden because she knew we'd follow. She's laying a trap."

Isabelle nodded. "All the more reason to move quickly. We don't know if she'll attack on arrival, or wait until you've got your guard down a bit. We don't even know if she'll be alone—there's a good chance she's got other demons lying in wait."

"An ambush," Gabriel said. "Excellent. So all we've got to do is hop on this magic portal-bus straight to hell, avoid detection at all costs, rescue the souls from some unknown secret location, assassinate the demonic reprobates, and catch a ride back before anyone finds out we were even there."

A nervous laugh bubbled up from Jaci's insides. "You make it sound like such a drag, Prince."

"Are you kidding me? Any date where I get to slit demon throats is a good one."

He touched the blade strapped under his shirt, and Jaci tried not to shiver.

He'd given her a quick history lesson about the demonic weapon after he'd gotten it from Dorian, but Jaci still didn't understand what it would actually do for them down in hell, or how they were supposed to get close enough to Viansa or Azerius to use it.

Apparently, Rogozin hadn't been all that forthcoming with the intel when he'd left it behind.

Aside from the blade, their only other weapon was a stash of devil's trap flash-bangs Isabelle had made—about a dozen small vials. Probably wouldn't kill any demons, but detonating one might buy them a few extra minutes to get out of a jam, should the need arise.

And in hell, the need would almost certainly arise.

"You can return through this same portal or, if you get separated, through any portal in hell," Isabelle said. "Just use your connection to Ravenswood to call you back here."

Jaci nodded. She and Gabriel were both carrying spelled dirt from the crypts—a grounding element that would create a magical tether to Ravenswood.

That was just a precaution, though. Ravenswood was where Gabriel's family lived. Where *Jaci's* family lived—a family that had chosen her, accepted her, darkness and all. Deep down, she knew they'd always find their way home, magic dirt or not.

"Before you two step back through," Isabelle continued, "you'll need to send the recovered souls ahead of you with a spell."

"A spell?" Gabriel asked. "Why's that?"

"My father and Aiden exist in hell as soul energy," Jaci said. "We'll experience them as physical beings because we shared connections to them in the physical realm, but they won't be able to step back through the portal on their own. Their bodies are still here, so we'll need to give them a magical push, so to speak."

"I'll be here waiting for them," Isabelle said. "The moment those souls come through, I'll guide them back into their bodies. Gently, of course."

Jaci glanced down at Aiden, then at the empty space where her father was supposed to be. When she and Gabriel stepped back through the portal with the souls, the bodies had to be close. Souls brought into the material plane needed the immediate anchor of a physical body, or they'd never be able to reunite, cursed to wander for eternity.

Or worse—they'd end up back in hell.

"He'll be here," Isabelle said. "Colin's close."

Jaci nodded, forcing herself to stay focused. Positive. After all, getting the souls back into their bodies was the easier part, especially for a witch with Isabelle's skills.

First, she and Gabriel had to find and rescue them.

If they couldn't, it wouldn't matter whether the bodies were here or in the hospital or rotting away in an unmarked grave.

Aiden and Zachary wouldn't stand a chance.

"And you two?" Dorian asked. "How will you get back after the souls are through?"

"If all goes according to plan," Jaci said, "Gabriel and I should be able to walk back through the portal just like we would any other door."

"Then we'll close it behind them by breaking the salt circle," Isabelle said. "That should sever the connection to hell."

Dorian sighed. "That's a few too many *shoulds* and *ifs* for my liking."

"Shoulds and ifs are all we've got at the moment," Jaci said. Then, offering what she hoped was an encouraging smile, "But a good witch always knows how to improvise."

"You *are* a good witch, moonflower," Gabriel said, and she smiled, buoyed by the vote of confidence. By his love. By his very presence.

"Listen, little miss hot-pants." Cole stepped up, hands on her shoulders. "You get into trouble out there—the kind where you just know you're in over your head—you fight like hell, hear me?"

"You know I will."

"None of this high-road, second-chances bullshit. Not everyone can be saved, and not everyone deserves to be redeemed." Cole stuck a cigarette in his mouth, but for once, he didn't light it. "Sometimes you just gotta put on your shit-stompin' boots and take out the damn trash. You get what I'm sayin'?"

"No one gets what you're saying, mate," Gabriel said. "You're high."

"It's a metaphor, Little Red. Keep up."

Gabriel laughed. "Doing my best, wolf."

Isabelle cleared her throat, her eyes dark and somber. "All right, everyone. It's time."

Careful not to disturb the salt circle, Gabriel and Jaci stepped inside the pentagram, then turned to face each other.

Gabriel reached for her hands. Brushed his thumbs over her knuckles.

"Partners," he whispered, his green eyes fierce in the flickering candlelight.

"Always," she said.

The crypts fell silent, and Isabelle began her incantation, slowly walking around the circle, her voice so soft Jaci couldn't even make out the words.

The flames grew taller, brighter. The air around them began to shimmer and swirl, and then, with a sound like the tearing of fabric, a crack appeared before them, pulsing with bright, silver-white light.

Jaci stretched out a hand, her fingertips barely brushing the edge. The portal's magic crackled and brightened, calling out to her own magic. Her fury. Her hellfire.

Her darkness.

It surged to life inside her, and she felt her eyes shift to black, the magic sizzling across her skin, her body adjusting to contain it.

Gabriel took her hand again. Brought his mouth to her ear. "I love you, witch-demon," he whispered. "Now and forever. Light or dark. You belong to me. Understand?"

Jaci nodded.

Gabriel nodded back.

And together, without so much as a backward glance, they stepped into the light.

CHAPTER EIGHTEEN

Jaci had never smelled such sweet, inviting air. Had never heard such beautiful birdsong. Had never so badly wanted to kick off her shoes and run barefoot through the soft green grass.

Her heart swelled just to look at it.

And as she and Gabriel stepped out of the portal and into a serene forest, that swollen heart dropped right into her stomach.

She knew, without a doubt, which realm of hell they'd traveled to.

Which realm Viansa had chosen to imprison the souls, her every move orchestrated to ensure Jaci's maximum torment.

"I have to admit," Gabriel said, taking in the scene. "Not quite how I pictured the fiery pits of your homeland. Perhaps the demons need a better PR manager."

A shiver rolled through her body, and she tucked in

closer, calming herself with his familiar scent. His heat. The grooves of his body that fit her so perfectly, it felt as if they were carved and sculpted just for her.

All of *that*, at least, was real.

She led him through a natural archway beneath a canopy of trees. Sunlight filtered through the leaves, dancing on the ground before them, and Jaci stuck out her hand as if she could catch the light.

"Hell rule number one," she said sadly. "The more beautiful and serene it appears, the more dangerous and deadly it is."

A warm breeze whispered through the trees, and Gabriel sighed right along with it. "So we're basically fucked. Is that what you're telling me?"

Jaci squeezed his arm. She wished she had better news, but there was no point in sugar-coating things now.

They were in hell, after all. It's not like either of them had been expecting rainbows and fucking unicorns.

Would've been nice, though.

"Aiden and my father," she said. "Their souls are in the Hall of Broken Mirrors."

"Broken Mirrors?"

"Look." Jaci gestured up ahead, where the trees gave way to a clearing and a stark, single-story building that seemed to stretch on forever in both directions, like a great white wall.

No windows. No pillars or turrets. Nothing to mar its gleaming exterior but a single red door at the very center.

There was no need for additional exits.

The souls who entered never left.

"And this… hall," Gabriel said. "It's… what, exactly?"

"It's bad, Gabriel. Really bad." Jaci let out a shaky breath, tears blurring her eyes.

Hell was full of tortures. Every soul locked in its unholy cages experienced them differently, but every soul experienced them fully—as an embodied, conscious, physical being capable of feeling the most extreme forms of physical and psychological pain.

For some, their eternity in hell consisted of physical tortures—burning, waterboarding, walking on broken glass, swallowing nails, dental work and surgery without anesthesia.

Others were caught in an endless nightmare, forced to outrun the most heinous monsters of the underworld night after night, no reprieve.

Many simply became trapped in their own personal hells, cursed to relive their most devastating losses, the most brutal tortures they'd endured in life.

But the worst realm of hell was the Hall of Broken Mirrors.

It consisted of a single corridor that stretched on for miles, its walls and ceiling covered with black mirrors of all shapes and sizes. Each mirror reflected a picture of serenity —the promise of an escape to a better place. They called to lost souls like ports in a storm, drawing them in until they could no more look away than they could escape their eternal sentence.

Soon, the scene in the mirror would shift, revealing the

ugly truth behind its beautiful pretense—a reflection of the soul's deepest inner darkness.

Unlike the realms that forced a soul to relive its worst eternal traumas, the Hall of Broken Mirrors trapped a soul in a perpetual loop of the very traumas it had inflicted upon itself in life—debilitating fear, self-loathing, worthlessness, crushing regret, private shame, the kind of guilt that ate through a body like battery acid.

Every terrible thing a person had ever believed about themselves, all the pain and anguish they'd shoved down and buried deep, all the rotten things festering at their very core, the Hall of Broken Mirrors unearthed.

It stripped away anything good, any glimmer of hope and love and peace a person had ever felt in life.

And it trapped that soul in its own endless, abject misery.

There were no guards. No torturers. Nothing physically barring their exit. Because hell's creators knew the truth:

Self-hatred was its own prison, every soul its own most sadistic warden.

Jaci explained all this to Gabriel, doing her best to cling to the rapidly dwindling hope in her heart as they walked through the clearing to the ominous red door.

Then, they stopped.

A tear slipped down her cheek as she imagined what they might find on the other side, and wordlessly, Gabriel slid his hands into her hair, pulling her head to his chest. His heartbeat thumped against her ear, a beat by which she steadied her own.

"Gabriel," she said softly. Reverently, as if this was a holy place. Hallowed ground.

"I'm here, moonflower. With you every step of the way."

"I know. It's just... Once a soul becomes trapped in the Hall of Broken Mirrors, the chance of them still recognizing us—let alone being strong enough to break the mirror's hold—is almost zero." She pulled back, gazed into his eyes. "We may not be able to save them."

"*Almost* zero, you say?" Gabriel let out a soft laugh, wiping away her tears with his thumbs. "Better than *actual* zero. I can work with those odds."

Jaci nodded, the tiniest smile touching her lips.

"Once we're in there, we'll need to draw them to us. I'll focus on my father, you focus on Aiden."

"Focus... as in, just think about him?"

"Yes. Picture him clearly in your mind. Try to call up a strong memory—an experience you shared. One that was equally resonant for you both."

Gabriel smirked. "Does it have to be a good memory?"

"Not necessarily, but... Knowing what I know about Aiden? I think he'd respond better to a good one."

"Yes, Vampire Ken has always been a bit of a sap." Gabriel's smirk faded into a warm smile, genuine affection shining in his eyes. "Don't worry. I've got just the thing."

"We'll need to walk the corridors—slowly, carefully—sending out our energy."

"How will we know when we've found them?"

"We'll feel them before we see them—like a tug or a rush of warmth. You'll know it when it happens. Then, we stop. Wait for them to come to us. We don't want to frighten them off." She squeezed his hand. "We're their beacons, Gabriel. We can't lose sight of that."

He nodded, suddenly very serious.

Then, she pushed open the door. "Whatever you do, do *not* look into the mirrors."

They stepped inside.

And what they saw there nearly brought her to her knees.

"Bloody hell, Jace." Gabriel gasped. "Are those… are they all…"

She nodded, unable to find words.

The hall was like a museum gallery, only instead of artwork, the cruel black mirrors were on full display.

Standing along the walls and floating near the ceiling, crowding into every available bit of space, the doomed souls stared into the mirrors with vacant eyes, hands pressed to the glass, twisted mouths stretched open in perpetual torment.

The corridor was soundless.

Jaci grabbed his hand, laced their fingers together. And slowly, step by step, they made their way down the center of the corridor.

While Gabriel thought of Aiden, Jaci called up a memory of her father—the last time she'd seen him wholly alive, soul intact, just after they'd arrived in New York.

She remembered the smell of pizza and pasta drifting on the air, the snowflakes she'd never before seen.

She remembered how they'd laughed and spun in circles in that alley, catching the snowflakes, finally free.

She didn't think about what had come after that. Just the best moments, the ones that she'd always carry with her, no matter what happened today.

I love you so much, Dad. Come back to me. Please come back to me. Let me take you home. Let me take you home…

She repeated the mantra in her mind, remembering the snow in Little Italy on their arrival, thinking of the snow at Ravenswood, wanting so badly to share it with him. Not just Ravenswood itself, but the Redthornes, her expanding family, her life. Her vampire prince.

Let me take you home…

Something brushed along the back of her neck, raising the hairs on her arms, making her heart flutter.

"I can feel him!" Jaci whispered. "Gabriel, he's close!"

She turned on her heel, slowly scanning the souls for a hint of familiarity, a glimpse of him, anything, and then…

"*Dad*," she breathed, and at her barest whisper, the man at the mirror beside her turned to face her.

His bight blue eyes had lost none of their luster, but his face held no expression, no hint that he had any idea the woman who stood before him was his daughter.

Jaci went as still as a statue on the outside, but inside, her heart jackhammered in her chest, her stomach tying itself into knots as she waited for even a *glimmer* of recognition in those blue eyes…

Her father shook his head. Closed his eyes. Let out a

long, slow breath that seemed to go on forever, as if he'd been holding it for the entire seven years they'd been apart.

"It's okay," Gabriel whispered beside her. "Give him a moment. Just a moment."

She nodded, knowing he was right, trusting it, but her whole body felt like a war zone.

Like if he didn't look at her again, say something, *do* something, she might explode.

Please, Dad, she thought. *Please.*

As if he'd heard her thoughts, her father opened his eyes. Met her gaze. Tears glazed his eyes, and behind them, she saw the dawn of memory rising once more and she knew—she *knew*—her father had finally come back to her.

"It's me, Dad," she whispered, her tears blurring the sight of him. "Jacinda. I've come to take you home."

He smiled and reached for her face, cradling it gently, shaking his head as if he couldn't believe it.

He opened his mouth, closed it again. Took a deep breath.

But still, he couldn't seem to find the words.

"It's okay," she said, touching her forehead to his. "It's over, Dad. It's okay."

Then, glancing up at Gabriel, she said softly, "Anything from Aiden?"

"Not yet. I think we should send your father back through the portal first, then come back for Aiden."

Jaci nodded. It could take hours to find another soul; she didn't want to keep her father here a moment longer.

Gabriel leaned in close, whispered into her hair. "Right behind you, little moonflower. Every step."

Wrapping an arm around her father's shoulders, borrowing a bit more courage from her vampire prince, she led him back down the corridor, out the red door, and through the canopy of trees so green they made her heart ache.

Tucked between two ponderosa pines, the portal they'd arrived through still glowed bright, as if it'd been waiting for them.

Jaci smiled, picturing Dorian and Isabelle on the other side, Colin, her father, all of them.

This was really happening. After twenty-five years in hell, Zachary Colburn was going home.

He still hadn't spoken, but he seemed to understand instinctively what was happening.

He stood before the portal, hands relaxed at his sides, calm and ready.

"I need to do a spell to send you back through," she explained. "You've got friends waiting for you on the other side to help guide you into your body. We'll be right behind you."

He nodded. Took a deep breath. Nodded again.

"Close your eyes, Dad." Jaci removed a bit of the Ravenswood dirt from her pocket and sprinkled it over his head.

Then, closing her eyes too, she conjured the image of the Eight of Knives, a Tarot card she'd drawn for Gabriel the very first time he'd sat across from her at the table in her apartment and demanded she break his curse.

It was a card of imprisonment, featuring a demonic beast chained to a wooden post in a poisonous swamp, ravens scavenging the bones of those that'd died before him.

Now, she imagined its reversal, visualizing the card being shredded into bits, breaking the dark magic that had trapped her father here for nearly half of his life.

She pictured the ravens taking flight, just as her father's soul would take flight, and the chains disintegrating in the poisonous waters, forever broken.

Then, her hands placed gently on his back, Ravenswood firmly in her mind, she uttered the spell that would end her father's eternal torment.

The spell that would send him home.

> *Eight of Knives, chained and broken*
> *What was lost has now been found*
> *By these words that I have spoken*
> *Free the soul that darkness bound*

By the time she finished her third recitation, Zachary Colburn was gone.

When she looked up at Gabriel again, her vampire smiled, the same tears glittering in his eyes that she felt in her own.

Without a word, he took her hand, and together they headed back through the archway.

Back to the red door.

She hoped Aiden might be waiting for them on the other side. That somehow, he'd picked up on Gabriel's thoughts.

But when they opened the door and stepped into the massive corridor once more, the soul awaiting them *wasn't* the sweet, handsome vampire who'd made her laugh in the Ravenswood study, teasing Gabriel and promising to give Jaci the full report about his sunrise coffee date with Sasha.

The soul awaiting them wasn't a soul at all.

He was a demon, dragged up from the very depths of hell, ancient and horrifying, reeking of brimstone and bloodlust and death.

The monster towered nearly ten feet high, with skin as translucent as rice paper stretched thin over a skeleton of sharp black bones.

He wore a crown of claws and teeth on his bald head, fused to the skin in parts, as if it were growing straight into his skull—or out from it.

His eyes, if he'd ever even had them, were gone, nothing but scarred flesh covering the dark pits in his skull.

His nose was a rotten hole, his mouth sewn shut with razor wire.

His body was little more than a skeleton frame draped in tattered, milky-white skin, cracked and bleeding, broken bones jutting out from his ribcage.

As Jaci and Gabriel stood before him, paralyzed by his very presence, the demon bowed his head in greeting.

Then, in an explosion of feathers and blood, two

massive white wings shot out from between his shoulder blades.

Jaci fell to her knees, blood leaking from her eyes and ears.

And deep inside her skull, the King of Blood and Ravens laughed.

CHAPTER NINETEEN

Ever since Jacinda told him how the Hall of Broken Mirrors worked, Gabriel had been expecting the child.

Though he hadn't looked upon the black mirrors, he knew—somehow—she was waiting for him.

And now, as they stepped through the red door in search of Aiden, there she was. Gazing up at him, haunted and broken as ever. Lost. As if Gabriel was supposed to do something about it. To have all the answers. To fix all the things he'd broken in his life.

Maybe this time, he could've tried.

Maybe this time, he *would* have tried.

But towering behind her, like a nightmare drudged up from the basement of his own private hell, was the demon Azerius.

Gabriel stopped breathing.

White wings exploded from the demon's body, and

Jacinda fell to her knees, blood running down her cheeks. Spilling in dark rivers from her ears.

"Will you let her die, vampire prince?" the child whispered. "Will you abandon your witch?"

All of Gabriel's worst fears rushed back to the surface, crashing through his mind in vivid detail, the terrible visions Viansa had ignited.

He'd watched Jacinda die a thousand times.

Kostya and He Who Likes to Watch, the fires of hell, Viansa, the dark mages, the stake driven by Gabriel's own hand, each death more gruesome than the last.

The demon's laughter rang out through Gabriel's skull, razor blades and claws. He clutched his head, trying to stop the echo, the splitting ache that blurred his vision.

"No," Gabriel gritted out. To the child. To the demon. To Jacinda herself. "I will not… let her… die."

The child vanished.

He fell to his knees beside Jacinda. Reached for her.

"Bow before me," Azerius demanded, the ringing of his voice like the end of the world. "Weep for the fallen, for I am the King of Blood and Ravens, He Who Slaughters the Blood of his Blood, He for Whom the Dark Flame Rises, and all who gaze upon my true form shall tremble before it and beg for death."

"Jacinda," Gabriel whispered, brushing the hair from her face. "Get up, love. You must get up. We have to go. Now."

She turned toward him and nodded, her eyes red with blood. He scented it, smoky and full adrenaline.

Gabriel swallowed his fear. Helped her to her feet.

No, he thought once more. *I will not let her die…*

"I'm Gabriel Redthorne," he said to the demon. "This is Jacinda Colburn. And I'm certain I speak for both of us when I say… You can fuck *right* off."

He grabbed Jacinda and blurred her down the corridor, past the black mirrors, past the souls who clung to them, oblivious to the terror in their midst.

Azerius followed in their wake, the tips of his massive wings knocking the mirrors from the walls. They hit the ground and shattered, sending the souls to their knees as they scrambled to pick up the broken shards.

Gabriel blurred them further down the corridor, but again, the demon followed.

"You can *not* win this battle, vampire prince," Azerius said. "You and the witch belong to me now. And as the dawn rises in your world once more, all those whom you have loved and despised alike will belong to me. The realm of mortals shall be no more."

Every word sliced through Gabriel's mind, the pain blinding him. Jacinda could hardly stand.

It was no use. They couldn't outrun him.

They had to fight.

Gabriel shoved Jacinda behind him and pulled the blade from its sheath. Before the monster could unleash another poisonous word, Gabriel attacked, slamming into his skeletal body with the strength and fury of a tempest.

He broke upon the demon like a wave against the shore,

retreating just as quickly. He'd scored a glancing blow off his thigh—barely a scratch.

Azerius laughed. "You think to harm me with my own blade? Your blood is tainted, vampire. Cursed. You have neither the strength nor the courage—"

Gabriel blurred back in the other direction, leading the demon away from Jacinda.

He felt the rush of air against his back as Azerius took the bait, racing toward him once more.

Gabriel spun on his heel, blurred in for another attack. He slammed a fist through Azerius's lower abdomen, but when he pulled back, there was only bone and ash. No blood. No guts. Nothing to rip out.

"Fool." Azerius laughed again and flapped his great wings. Batted Gabriel's body like a cat toying with a mouse, slamming him to the ground.

Gabriel scrambled to his feet, gripped the bone-handled blade, and tried again. Again. Again. His best attacks were no more than an annoyance to the ancient demon, and he was quickly losing steam, his wounds slow to heal, heart pounding so hard he feared it might burst.

Another blow. Another miss. Another skull-splitting speech from the fearsome demon determined to live up to every last one of his names, Gabriel fell to his knees.

Hope evaporated from his heart. Dorian had bested Azerius on that rooftop in New York, but here, there was no vessel to fight—no weak human, no equally matched vampire, no shifter Gabriel might overcome with speed and strength.

This was Azerius in his true form. Unbeatable. Unbreakable.

The child flickered to life once more.

"Your death," she whispered through a menacing smile, "will be her undoing."

The words ignited his rage once more, and Gabriel shot to his feet, blurring into Azerius with a roar that rattled the few mirrors still hanging on the walls.

"You will *burn*!" he shouted, sinking the blade deep in the demon's side.

But Azerius would not go down.

"This is where we part ways, vampire. I shall give your brother your regards."

Gabriel jerked the knife free and readied himself for another go, but before he could make a move, Azerius wrapped a bony hand around his throat, lifting him off the ground and bringing him level with that eyeless, hideous face.

With a cruel, mocking laugh, Azerius said, "Oh, how I look forward to the pleasure of recalling this moment for King Dorian. Right before I snap him in half, just as I'm going to do to you."

"Oh, I think the fuck *not*, He Who Haveth Dick for Brains."

Jacinda.

She stood behind Azerius with her hands raised, hellfire surging in one, a half-dozen glass vials clutched in the other.

Gabriel met her gaze. The fire. The determination. The badassery he'd fallen in love with from the very start.

He nodded once.

And Jacinda pitched the vials to the ground at the demons feet, blasting him with a ball of silver-blue hellfire that surged across his wings.

He dropped Gabriel and spun around to face his new attacker, and Gabriel blurred to her side, blade raised once more.

But the attack never came.

Azerius was immobilized, his wings smoking and singed, his black heart glowing with dark fire behind his thin skin, limbs twitching as Isabelle's devil's traps slowly took hold.

Jacinda hit him with another blast of hellfire, dropping him to his knees with a force that shook the floor.

Still, Azerius laughed. "You think yourself clever, witch-demon, but your time with the humans has made you soft and weak. This pathetic magic won't bind me for long."

"Ehh, you're probably right." Jacinda glanced at Gabriel, then down at the blade still clutched in his hand. Then, with a grin that sent all that lost hope surging back into Gabriel's heart with a vengeance, she turned to Azerius and said, "But *this* will, you eyeless, dickless cunt."

She raised her hands once more. The hellfire surged in her palms, surged from Azerius's wings, magic gathering around her like the fiercest storm.

Then, she called out her spell.

King of Blood and Ravens, demon of the deep
No longer shall we tremble, no longer shall
    we weep
By the power of the Knives, to this blade I bind you
Back to darkness you return, where none shall ever
    find you

The last line echoed down the corridor, and Azerius roared in pain.

"What have you done?" he shouted. "What is this madness? I am the Demon For Whom the World Shall Burn! The King of—"

"Now, Gabriel!" Jacinda shouted. "Do it!"

At his witch's command, Gabriel blurred into Azerius one more time, shoving the blade deep into his heart.

The dark flame inside flickered, then sputtered out.

The hellfire receded from his wings.

The tattered remains of his skin smoked and curled away from the bone, blowing away like ashes from burning wood.

The black skeleton splintered and cracked, bones falling to the ground like broken glass.

Gabriel blinked away the shock. Turned to his woman. Saw the tears in her eyes, the smile on her face, and he reached for her.

But then, just as his fingers brushed her moonlight hair, a deep rumble shook the ground, and the Hall of Broken Mirrors exploded.

When Gabriel opened his eyes again, he was flat on his back, the air pressed from his lungs. He looked up into the smoky red haze of a different sky, a different realm.

And he knew, before he'd even taken his first breath, Jacinda was gone.

CHAPTER TWENTY

Jaci had been walking for years.

That's how it felt.

Her feet bled, every step sending a bright burst of pain through her legs, but she didn't dare stop.

Something awaited her at the end of all this. Something she needed to find and face.

Viansa.

Azerius was gone, bound to the very weapon he'd created, bound to all the dark, demonic souls it had imprisoned, but Jaci knew hell wouldn't release her from its clutches until she settled this.

Ended it.

Another shock of pain reverberated through her bones, but she pressed on, one foot in front of the other.

She knew exactly where she was.

The Labyrinth.

It was an endless maze, each twist and turn forking into

a hundred more. Some paths were made of ice cliffs so high, one misstep promised a fall into a bottomless winter void. Others passed through poisonous waters that melted the skin from your bones.

Only one would lead her to the center. Only one would deliver her from this death sentence.

Like everything else about this journey, the trip through the Labyrinth was orchestrated by Viansa—some new torment to entertain the bitch.

Ironically, Jaci had walked these roads so many times— often to escape her sister, other times at her sister's command—she knew each one by heart. Knew exactly where to turn, where to duck. When to tiptoe and when to run.

So onward she marched, through treacherous pathways beneath even more treacherous skies, until—bleeding and winded, eyes stinging, mouth so dry she was ready to bite her wrist and suck out her own blood—she finally reached the center.

The Heart of Flames.

The very core of hell itself.

She stepped through an archway of fire into a cavern as black as night, the only light a faint red glow around the perimeter, pulsing like a heartbeat. Heat rose from the ground. A trickle of sweat raced down her back.

Jaci closed her eyes. Took a deep breath.

"Viansa," she whispered. "I can hear you breathing, succubus."

Footsteps echoed off the cavern floor, and Jaci finally opened her eyes.

Her sister stood before her, arms folded over her chest, hair and face as glossy and perfect as always.

With a dark grin, Viansa looked her over and said, "Been a minute, Lab Rat."

"Has it? I wasn't counting. I was too busy saving my father's soul and executing your fearless leader who, as it turns out, cries like a little bitch when he's beaten."

"So hard to find good demonic warlords these days." Viansa sighed and rolled her eyes. "Suppose I'll have to keep looking."

"Or you could, I don't know. Stop this takeover bullshit and focus on getting your shit together? Face it, girl. You're a hot mess."

"Says the witch who can't fight a battle without her vampire boyfriend at her side?" Viansa laughed. "At least I'm an independent woman."

"Who kidnaps innocent souls just to get the attention of her sister? Please. You're as dependent as they come."

"If you're talking about my little non-consensual road trip with Aiden Donovan, I wasn't trying to get your attention. I simply wanted you to come back home so we could figure this thing out together. And look!" She beamed, spreading her hands before her. "Here you are."

"Here I am."

"Sisters, reunited. So… Let's say we put all this nastiness behind us and start fresh. Water under the bridge, right?"

Jaci stared at her, incredulous.

Water under the bridge?

Viansa had colluded with their mother, helping the woman drug and rape Jaci's father just so they could conceive their own little hybrid hellbeast. After Jaci was born, Viansa appointed herself tormentor-in-chief, abusing her—literally torturing her—for eighteen years. She'd crashed back into her life a couple of months ago, wreaking havoc on the city where Jaci had made her life, threatening everyone Jaci had come to care about. She'd imprisoned Zachary's soul. Stolen Aiden's.

And now she wanted to shove it all under the bridge?

Jaci circled her, the heat of the cavern mingling with her anger, making her blood simmer.

On some level, Jaci would always be terrified of Viansa. But now, here, after everything she'd endured, she realized her final reckoning—the most terrifying fear she had to face and accept—wasn't about Viansa at all.

It was about her own darkness. Her own capacity for violence and rage.

During the slaughter at Shimmer and again at Renault's warehouse, it was the death energy of the murdered mages that'd fueled Jaci's most destructive powers. She'd always assumed it was the magic itself that'd connected her to them—after all, the same dark magic that ran through their blood also ran through hers.

But now, glaring at the succubus who'd made her life a literal hell, Jaci realized her powers had nothing to do with the mages and everything to do with the darkness itself.

With *her*.

It wasn't some external power, but a thing that existed inside her—a living, breathing entity that was just as much a part of her as her blue eyes and silvery hair. And here, in the darkest, most malicious realm of the universe—the place of her creation, her birth, and her entire childhood—she finally understood what she had to do.

Embrace it.

Claim herself.

Fucking *own* it—no apologies, no excuses.

With a calmness that belied the new flutter in her heart, Jaci smiled and lifted her hands, calling another Tarot card to her mind.

Temperance—an ethereal queen of the night in a black lace dress, black wings unfurling behind her. In one hand, she clutched a bloody arrow, and in the other, a chalice of blood tipping into a flaming cauldron. Roses bloomed at its base.

It was a card of alchemy and self-acceptance, a melding of the light and the dark, of earth and hell, of angels and demons, of all the things that made Jaci who she was.

And she was done trying to choose between them. Done pretending she even wanted to.

"What... what are you doing?" Viansa asked, a hint of fear cracking her voice.

In response, Jaci grinned, and the spell came to her at once, flowing from the very center of her being, up through her heart and lungs, out through her lips and into the air around her, filling hell's Heart of Flames with her magic. Her essence.

Blood and fire, breath and blade
Broken fragments now remade
Light to darkness, dark to light
Bow before the queen of night

A hot wind blew through the cavern, and the magic surged inside her, hollowing her out, chipping and scraping and sucking until she felt like an empty vessel waiting to receive. And then, in a sudden rush of pure, white-hot energy, it filled her all over again.

Her body buzzed like a live wire, every cell vibrating, tiny arcs of lightning zig-zagging across her skin. It was like that night in the warehouse, only bigger, vaster, her whole being full of potential so awesome and terrifying, it brought tears to her eyes.

Before her, Viansa's eyes widened, black hair whipping around her face, her lithe body barely able to stand upright inside the tempest of Jaci's unfathomable power.

"Quit fucking around, Lab Rat!" Viansa shouted. She tried to call up her hellfire, but in the wake of Jaci's magic, it fizzled in her hands. "I mean… Sorry. *Jacinda.*"

"No, Lab Rat is just fine," Jaci said. "I *am* a lab rat. A creation forged in hell. *This* is what you and our mother made. And *this* is the fate you brought upon yourself."

She lifted her hands once more. Let the hellfire dance between them, the magic swirling around her. And then, for just a moment, she looked deep into the eyes of the so-called sister who'd never known the true meaning of family, willing herself to find even a *modicum* of sympathy.

"Please," Viansa whispered, her eyes flooding with genuine tears. Maybe even a hint of regret.

There was a time when Jaci might've given in. Tried to talk things out.

But like Cole said, not everyone could be saved. Not everyone deserved to be redeemed.

Sometimes, you just had to put on your shit-stomping boots and take out the damn trash.

Jaci shook her head. Smiled one last, brilliant, star-bright smile for Viansa—the last thing the succubus would ever see.

And then, she unleashed hell.

The magic flowed through her palms, slamming into Viansa's chest in a burst of silver and blue hellfire.

It split the succubus in two, melting the skin from her body, boiling her blood, setting her bones on fire.

It was terrible and gruesome. The smell of death nearly overwhelmed her.

But Jaci didn't let up.

For her father, for Aiden, for Gabriel, for all the innocent humans Viansa had killed in New York, she didn't let up.

For herself, she didn't let up. Not until her limbs trembled and her magic fizzled and she barely had the strength to stand.

~

In the end, there was nothing left of the demon. Not even a pile of ash. Not even a shadow. Not even a memory.

Viansa, terrorizer of New York City, goddess among mages, hijacker of minds, original succubus, first of her kind, was finally gone.

And Jaci, conjurer of darkness, witch-demon-hybrid lab rat, plant-whisperer, and kickass bartender to the supernatural elite, had never felt so fucking alive.

CHAPTER TWENTY-ONE

Gabriel couldn't decide which was worse—the incessant ringing in his head, the acrid smell of charred demon flesh searing his lungs, or the blood-red smirk of the female demon in a blue pinstripe suit, glaring down at him from atop a pile of smoldering bones.

Behind her, the child hovered close, haunting as ever.

He got to his feet, tried to shake off the ringing. It faded a bit, but left a monstrous fucking headache behind, so intense it made him dizzy.

And speaking of fucking headaches…

"Gabriel Redthorne," the demoness purred, carefully picking her way through the bones in a pair of spiked red heels. If she noticed the child following her, she didn't acknowledge it. "Young prince of House Redthorne, son of the fallen king, brother to the new. At this rate, I'll have the complete set in no time."

Fuck.

The woman needed no introduction. One look at that raven hair, and Gabriel knew.

"Ah, the *mother*," he said with a sneer. "I'd hoped we might pass through unmolested by the likes of you."

"The mother?" She waved away the word, batting her long lashes. "So cold and unfeeling. I have a name, vampire."

"I'm sure you do. Now, if you'll excuse me…" He stalked past her and climbed up onto another pile of bones the size of a small hill, hoping to get a better vantage point.

The mother and child followed, close as shadows.

Gabriel did his best to ignore them both, turning his attention to the wide expanse that now surrounded him.

The gleaming white halls where they'd fought Azerius only moments earlier had vanished. He saw nothing more than a fiery wasteland now, no landmarks to differentiate one direction from the other, nothing but smoke and bones as far as the eye could see.

"Jacinda!" he shouted. "Jacinda!"

But there was no reply. Not even an echo of his own desperate calls.

"She can't hear you, young prince." The mother linked her arm through his. "Why don't we go somewhere a little less… apocalyptic. My place, perhaps? I'll fix you a drink, and you can fill me in on everything I've missed about my daughter's life on the outside."

"I'm not going anywhere with you, demon."

"Well, not with *that* attitude, you're not." She laughed, low and throaty. "You and Jacinda have only just arrived, so

I understand things are a bit… disorienting. But that will change once you've settled in. Better to make friends than enemies, no?"

"We're not staying," he said firmly.

Behind her, the ghost-girl laughed, a silent rasp he felt rather than heard. Goosebumps erupted across his scalp.

"Hmm. Pity." The mother frowned, raking her gaze down to Gabriel's feet, then back up. "It's true, though. I have no official claim on your soul—not until your death. But Jacinda? She's my daughter."

"Not anymore." Gabriel scurried back down the hill of bones. He had no idea where the fuck he was going, but he needed forward momentum in some direction—*any* direction. As long as it was away from the mother and that cursed child, that's all that mattered.

"Where are you off to?" The mother asked. She was practically on top of him again, her movements quick and silent. Horrifying, though he refused to reveal how badly her presence made his skin crawl.

More, even, than the child. Gabriel had gotten used to her, at least. The hollow eyes. The bloody dress. The accusations burning through his gut at her very presence.

But the demon was worse. Not because she was a powerful original. Not because she'd tortured and abused her daughter.

But because her very presence here made the base of his skull itch, as if something were trying to claw its way out. To warn him.

What the bloody hell does this bitch want?

"I need to find Jacinda," he said.

"You won't find her over there." Like smoke, she slipped around from behind him to stand in front of him, hands on her hips, that hideous painted smirk stretched wide across her face.

"Where is she?" he demanded.

"I imagine she'll be along soon. She and Viansa are in the Labyrinth—seems they've got some things to work out. Sisters, you know." She rolled her eyes. "Ah, the drama. The two of them have quite a history."

The Labyrinth. Gabriel had no idea what the fuck it meant, but it certainly didn't sound like the kind of place you wanted to be trapped in with the evil succubus who'd been torturing you since birth and actively trying to kill you for weeks.

Tamping down the fresh terror surging inside, he said, "Tell me how to get there."

"*You* can't get there." She turned and glanced out across the wasteland. Far in the distance, red lightning sizzled on the horizon, illuminating the black clouds overhead. "When Azerius died, the blast caused some sort of ripple effect. It tore the veils between hell's realms, creating temporary access points to areas most of us haven't visited in millennia. Viansa took her sister to one such place. You, on the other hand, ended up here."

"Where are these access points? I need to get—"

"Closed, I'm afraid. Like I said—the tearing of the veils was temporary. An unintended consequence of Azerius' little…" She spread her fingers and puffed out her cheeks, imitating an explosion.

"But you know where Jacinda is? Know for a fact she's with Viansa?"

"Hell is my home, vampire. My domain. I sense the souls of all who pass through my gates, whether they intend it or not. My daughters? I know where they are. Always."

Icy dread settled into his gut at that, but again, Gabriel refused to show the bitch even a hint of fear.

"So Azerius is truly dead?" he asked. "Not just banished or… I don't know. Blasted through one of the veils into another realm?"

"Not to put too fine a point on it," she replied, glancing at her glossy black fingernails, "but your trick with the blade essentially blasted him into his own asshole. So yes, Azerius—King of Blood and Ravens, He Whom Before All Mortals Weep, He Who Has Too May Damn Names to Remember—is truly dead."

A wave of relief washed over Gabriel, a modicum of tension easing from his shoulders.

He wouldn't fully relax until he had Jacinda back in his arms and they'd safely returned to Ravenswood, but if the mother was telling the truth about Azerius, that was certainly cause for celebration. A deep breath, at the very least.

"You don't seem all that broken up about it," he said.

"Azerius? Please. His 'burn first, ask questions never' policy is the reason we've been stuck here for untold millennia. If that demon had shown even a shred of diplomacy just *one* time in his entire cursed existence..." She glanced up at Gabriel, her grin stretching wide once more. "Well. You and I would be having this conversation in *your* backyard rather than mine."

"Doubtful."

She shrugged and returned her attention to her fingernails. "Anyway, unless you've got another demonic nuke up your sleeve, I'm afraid we'll just have to wait her out. She'll be along eventually. Seems she can't stay away from *you* for very long, devil only knows why. Personally, I find your company quite dreadful."

"The feeling is mutual, I assure you. And while I'm more than happy to wait her out, there's no need for you to do the same. Jacinda and I are leaving the moment she gets back."

"Leaving?" Her mouth rounded in shock, as if the idea of Jacinda wanting to escape this place was the craziest notion the bitch had ever heard. "Surely Jacinda will want to see her mother."

"Sorry, mum. No time for teary family reunions. So feel free to fuck off back to whatever hole you slithered out of and leave us both in peace."

She folded her arms across her chest, anger flickering in her eyes. "I *will* see my daughter, vampire. We haven't even exchanged a single word in seven years."

"She'll send you a postcard when she gets back home."

"Home?" The demoness threw her head back and laughed again, but this one wasn't flirtatious. This one slithered down his spine like a hundred serpents, the itch at the base of his skull turning into a burn. "Oh, you poor dear. Didn't she tell you about the contract?"

The word sent Gabriel's heart into overdrive. "Contract?"

"Even if I wanted to let her leave, I can't." The mother shrugged. "Rules are rules."

"You just told me you haven't exchanged so much as a word with her in years. How the bloody hell did she manage to sign a contract?"

"*She* didn't sign it. Her father did."

"You don't mean…" His mind raced, trying to figure out what the hell she was on about. What was it Jacinda had said about her last day here? "The deal her father made to save her when she turned eighteen? His soul for her freedom?"

"Ah, so she *did* tell you."

"That deal was honored seven years ago."

Her eyes shone with malice. Victory. "Was it?"

"Speak plainly, demon, for fuck's sake."

"You know what they say. The devil is in the details." She looped an arm through his again and sighed, as if this news pained her as much as it was about to pain him. "The terms were clear. Jacinda would only earn her freedom if her father pledged his eternal soul to me in hell. Unfortunately, he's no longer in hell, is he?"

"You have got to be fucking *kidding* me."

"It's a binding agreement, vampire. You know, as difficult as it is to watch your child leave the nest, I do realize

Jacinda is a grown woman now. It's not a mother's place to interfere with her daughter's choices at this stage of life. At the same time, the bond between a mother and child will always outlast any other. A mother sacrifices so much just to bring her child into this world. I don't expect you to understand—vampires can't produce offspring, of course. But being a parent... Well, it certainly gives you a whole new perspective on eternity..."

The woman went on waxing poetic about motherhood, but Gabriel was no longer listening, every word evaporating in the smoky air while the pain in his head intensified, leaking down into his heart.

More than anything, he wished he still had the Blade of Azerius. Wished he could bind her, smite her, exorcise her, *anything* to render this so-called contract null and void and protect the woman he loved from so much as one more terrible *second* in this woman's presence.

His fangs sliced through his gums, piercing his lower lip, drawing blood. His heart continued to pound its furious beat. His hands trembled and itched with the need to wrap around this woman's throat and press the bloody life out of her...

But then, amid his dark and fiery rage, an image flickered into view in Gabriel's mind, and all that red-hot anger evaporated.

A memory.

A party. Gabriel, hiding outside, avoiding his brothers and a manor full of guests.

And Jacinda, bonded witch to Renault Duchanes,

kneeling in the dirt in the gardens at Ravenswood. The moonlight shimmered in her hair, and the sight of her— ethereal, beautiful, mysterious, blooming in the darkness like a secret only he would ever know—it damn near stopped his heart, then and now.

Little moonflower…

He closed his eyes and held onto that image, burned it right into his soul.

He recalled her fierce determination, her refusal to break even in the midst of his cruel interrogation.

Recalled her courage in the face of all the shit that'd befallen them since.

Recalled the way she dove in front of that stake to save Charlotte—a woman she'd barely known at the time.

Recalled the way she'd charged into that warehouse to rescue Cole with nothing but her magic and the barest shred of hope.

Recalled her smile, the one that lit him up every time he caught even the barest glimpse of it.

And he recalled, in vivid, excruciating, heartbreaking detail, the taste of her kiss—the first one in his bed the morning after Shimmer, the last one still lingering on his lips.

Gabriel didn't want to live in a world without her. *Couldn't* live in a world without her.

But he couldn't allow the world to suffer that fate, either. The world *needed* Jacinda Colburn. And Gabriel needed to know that she was there, whole and alive, crafting magic and whispering to plants and mixing killer cocktails. Giving hell to anyone who dared cross her. Fighting the fight he sensed was only just beginning.

Gabriel opened his eyes and looked at the demoness. The mother of the woman he'd carve out his own heart—damn his own soul—to protect.

And he knew, in that moment, there was only one thing left to do.

"You say there's a contract," he said now, and the woman nodded, her eyes alight with sudden intrigue. Gabriel stepped closer. Held her gaze. Grinned—one that was sure to be his last. "Well. What if I made you a better offcr?"

CHAPTER TWENTY-TWO

Another hot wind. A final surge of magic. A blinding flash of light.

And Jaci stumbled out of the Heart of Flames and into the Hall of Broken Mirrors.

She gave herself a quick once-over—nothing bleeding, nothing broken, everything where it should be.

It was more than she could say for the corridor. The place was decimated, nothing left but a few pieces of white wall jutting up from the earth like broken teeth. Shards of black mirrors lay scattered at her feet. A few souls remained, sifting through the rubble.

Jaci waded through the remnants of the endless hallway, desperately searching for her prince, but aside from the souls, she was alone.

"Gabriel?" she called out. "Gabriel?"

No response.

Panic crawled up her throat. How had she ended up

back here without him? Had he been blasted to another realm as well? Did he know how to get back?

"Gabriel!" she cried out.

This time, she got a response.

"Jay-Jay?" came the call, clear and true, so familiar it made her heart ache.

No… It can't be…

Jaci raced toward the sound.

And there, stepping out from behind a hunk of blasted wall, was another demon. One with a recently shorn head, a fuzz of new hair just starting to grow back.

New *purple* hair.

"Meech?" Jaci laughed, joy and relief slamming into her chest, the force of both nearly knocking her on her ass. She ran to her cousin, crushing her in a breathless hug. "Meech! Seven hells, you're alive!"

"As far as I can tell, yeah. Wasn't sure for a minute there."

"What happened to you? I thought Viansa… She had your hair, Meech. Your hair!" Jaci pulled back, ran a hand over Meech's fuzzy head.

"She got me pretty good, girl." Meech blew out a breath. "When I heard she finally figured out how to manifest, I confronted her. Let's just say it wasn't my best idea. Got my ass beat up and locked in a coffin, dropped at the bottom of the Sea of Blood."

"Holy shit."

"Viansa and Azerius—she's working with that fucker— they had this whole plan, and the—"

"Azerius is dead. They're both dead. They're..." Jaci closed her eyes, forcing her thoughts to slow. "Damn it, Meech. So much has happened."

Fresh tears sprung to her eyes as she told Meech the story, the relief washing over her in waves as she recounted the battle with Azerius, the trip through the Labyrinth, her final moments with Viansa.

"That explains how I got out, then," Meech said. "When you killed Viansa, the magic she bound me with died right along with her. One minute I was in that box, and then... Poof. I'm here, looking for *your* crazy ass."

"Wait... the magic..." Jaci gasped, the realization finally dawning.

Viansa was truly dead.

Her magic was gone.

Which meant the Redthorne curse—the curse Viansa had bound all those centuries ago—was finally broken.

"Gabriel," she breathed. "He's okay. He's going to be okay."

Meech wrinkled her nose. "The vampire who kidnapped you?"

"Detained her," came the smooth reply from behind her, his voice close to her ear. Male. British. Sexy as sin. "Kidnapped is a bit harsh, don't you think?"

A shiver worked its way down Jaci's spine, and she turned to face him, the rush of emotions making her giddy.

Gabriel drew her close, buried his face in her hair. "Thank the devil you're safe, moonflower."

"Gabriel, the curse. It's broken. Viansa's dead and..."

Jaci pulled back to look at him again, the story spilling from her in a rush.

He cupped her face, his eyes shining with pride. Love. Wonder. All of it.

"You're incredible," he whispered.

"So you're the vampire who's got my girl all tied up in knots, huh?" Meech grinned, her gaze trailing down Gabriel's body, then back up.

"Gabriel Redthorne." He tipped his head and smiled. Dazzling. Heartbreaking. "Demetria, I presume. Glad to see you're still among the living."

"Gabriel. Like the angel, huh?"

"Bit more like the devil, I'm afraid."

"Mmm. Yummy." Meech glanced at Jaci, then back to Gabriel, then back to Jaci once more. "Don't suppose you're into sharing this one?"

"Not on your undead life, demon." Jaci turned to meet Gabriel's gaze once more, and he smiled at her and set her soul on fire. "Gabriel, the curse is broken. You're free. Dorian, Colin, Charlotte, Aiden, you're all—oh, shit. *Aiden*."

She spun on her heel, suddenly frantic. In the craziness of everything that'd gone down with Viansa, she'd nearly forgotten about the soul they'd yet to rescue.

"We need to find him," she said.

"Jacinda." Gabriel cupped her face once more, his breath warm on her lips. "He's here. Close. I can sense him, just like you said."

"Um, guys?" Meech nodded behind them, and Gabriel and Jaci turned.

"Aiden," Jaci breathed, unable to hide her relief.

He approached them slowly, his hands trembling, eyes wide with shock.

Gabriel laughed. "Aiden *bloody* Donovan. Never thought I'd say this, mate, but you were right. I fucking missed you." He pulled Aiden into a hug. "And I'm really not keen to do it again, so if you don't mind—"

"I'm… sorry." Aiden pulled out of the embrace, shaking his head. His eyes were haunted. Terrified.

"Aiden?" Gabriel asked.

Aiden blinked. Looked down at his hands in horror. "There was so much blood and I… I couldn't…" When he glanced up at them again, his face turned pale, his voice dropping to a whisper. "What have I done?"

"He doesn't recognize us," Jaci said. Then, to Aiden, "You haven't done anything, Aiden. Just got a bit lost is all. But we're here to take you home."

"But… Home?"

Jaci nodded, forcing a smile despite the fear racing through her limbs.

"To your brothers," she said gently.

"I've got brothers?"

"What's happened to him?" Gabriel whispered.

"Shock," Meech said. "Temporary memory loss. Should be fine once you get him topside, back into his body."

"Yes, you've got brothers," Jaci said softly. "Dorian, Colin—"

"Me," Gabriel said. "I'm right here, Aiden. It's Gabriel —remember?"

223

He blinked up at Gabriel, the barest flicker of recognition in his eyes. "Mac?"

Gabriel's face fell. "No, Mac isn't—"

"Mac isn't here right now," Jaci said, shooting Gabriel a warning glare. The last thing they needed to do was further upset him by telling him the only brother he remembered by name had died months earlier. "But yes, Mac—Malcolm —he's also your brother. Do you remember?"

Aiden nodded, some of the confusion clearing. "And my brothers… They're home? Waiting for me, you say?"

"At Ravenswood Manor," Gabriel said. "Upstate New York. It's December, and the grounds are beautiful—a winter wonderland. Dorian and Charlotte are planning a wedding."

"Charlotte… D'Amico," Aiden said.

"Yes! Yes, exactly." Gabriel touched his shoulder. "Cole's there too. Do you remember him?"

"Does he smoke?"

Gabriel laughed. "Like a fucking chimney."

Jaci blinked away the last of her tears.

Aiden was going to be okay. The curse was broken. They just needed to get back home.

Gently, carefully, they led him out of the rubble, Meech accompanying them back through the forest. The portal awaited, seemingly undisturbed by everything that'd happened.

"And you'll be joining me?" Aiden asked. "With my brothers at Ravenswood?"

Jaci smiled. "Absolutely."

This seemed to satisfy him, and he finally stepped in front of the portal.

Not wanting to wait another second, she sprinkled the dirt over his head and repeated the same spell she'd used on her father, giving Aiden a gentle nudge.

He disappeared into the light.

Another wave of relief crashed over her, and she looked at Gabriel with tears in her eyes, her throat tight.

"We did it," she whispered, a smile breaking across her face. "We saved them. We broke the curse and took down Azerius and... Holy hell, Gabriel. We really did it."

"*You* did it, little moonflower. As I knew you would."

"I couldn't have, though. Not without you. You—"

"Oh, please." Meech laughed and rolled her eyes. "You two are just about the most vomit-inducing thing I've ever seen, which is saying a lot, considering I'm one of the best torturers in the realm. But also... *Ugh*. Okay, fine. I'm here for it. Carry on. Feel free to use tongue this time."

"And she's your *favorite* relative?" Gabriel asked with a grin. "Bloody hell, woman. Perhaps we should stay in the pits a while, see if we can dredge up another one. Second-cousin, perhaps."

Meech folded her arms over her chest and huffed. "I'm letting you get away with that on account of your super-hotness. But if you keep pushing me, vampire—"

"Wouldn't dream of it, demon." He granted Meech one last smile, then grabbed Jaci's hand, glancing toward the portal. "Jace, we should probably..."

Jaci nodded.

Time to go.

She turned to her cousin, leaning in for another hug.

"Safe travels, Jay-Jay," Meech said. "Hit me up as soon as you get settled—we've still got a *lot* of catching up to do."

"Does this mean I can summon you again? You're back on the grid?"

"Hell yeah, I am. And I've got some time to make up for too. New tortures to devise, new demon boy-toys to torment. Big plans, girl. Big plans."

With a final kiss on the cheek for each of them, Meech was off, leaving Jaci and Gabriel alone once more.

"You ready to go home?" she asked him.

"More than I've ever been."

"Then let's—"

"Jacinda, wait. I need... I need to tell you something. I..." Gabriel trailed off, his eyes filling with longing. Sadness, even. He held her gaze another beat, thumb brushing across her mouth, but before she could ask him what he'd meant to say, he claimed her in a fiery kiss.

When he finally pulled away, his smile was firmly back in place.

"Me too, Prince," she said with a laugh. "Me too."

Jaci took his hand, and together, once more, they stepped into the light.

"They're back," Isabelle said. "They're back!"

Jaci pressed a hand to her chest, steadying her heartbeat as the scene came into focus.

Ravenswood. The crypts. The entire Redthorne clan gathered before them, along with Charley, Sasha, Cole, and Isabelle.

"Deep breaths," Colin was saying. "Can you hear me, Mr. Colburn?"

Jaci barely had enough time to get her bearings—to take in the welcoming, familiar faces, to see her father and Aiden sitting upright against the far wall as Colin checked their vitals—when she realized something was wrong.

Very wrong.

A sharp tug on her hand. A pained cry.

And Gabriel collapsed to the ground.

"Gabriel!" She fell to her knees, gathering him close. Holding him as he gasped for air, reaching for her face with a trembling hand.

Seven years vanished in a blink, and once again, Jaci was back in that alley in Little Italy, watching the light leave her father's eyes.

But this time, it wasn't her father. This time, the man taking his dying breath in her arms wasn't a man at all.

It was her vampire prince.

"No," she gasped, panic damn near choking her. "No, no, no… Gabriel! Wake up. Seven *hells*, please wake up!"

"What's wrong?" Isabelle knelt beside them, taking one of Gabriel's hands in hers. "Gabriel. What is it?"

Gabriel tried to smile. Blood leaked from his mouth. "Only way to save the… damsel."

"Shh. Don't talk." Jaci forced a smile, her mind racing. Had he been poisoned? Had something happened on their way back through the portal?

Gabriel touched her face. "I'm… sorry. I was wrong. I said death… but it's… you… Love. Moonflower."

He was fading. Babbling. Dying. They'd fought their way through hell and back, and now he was fucking *dying*.

"Gabriel, wait!" she cried, tears spilling as he stiffened in her arms. "Don't go. I can't do this without you. I can't… Don't leave me. Please don't leave me. *Please*…"

"Colin," Isabelle shouted. "Come quickly."

But Jaci knew it was too late.

She pressed her hand to Gabriel's heart. Felt the emptiness there. Felt the tug of his soul tearing free from his body, and knew in a matter of seconds he'd turn into ash.

Her tears splashed onto his face, but she knew he couldn't feel them.

Gabriel Redthorne, the vampire prince, the man she loved with her entire being, the man who'd followed her to hell and back, was already gone.

CHAPTER TWENTY-THREE

Emptiness.

It stretched on in all directions—a black void with neither end nor beginning.

Gabriel had no idea whether he was outside or in, dead or alive, forgotten in one of hell's lost, inaccessible realms or trapped in between hell and… somewhere else.

Purgatory?

He shook his head and sighed. Perhaps the answers existed only in the fine print on the demon deal he'd signed in haste—a mystery never to be solved.

The ground felt solid beneath his feet, though it looked no different than the space above him. Around him.

So, absent a better option, Gabriel did the only thing he could.

Walked.

For hours. Days, perhaps, with not so much as the glimmer of a single star to break the endless black.

He didn't hunger or thirst. Didn't tire. Didn't do anything but ache.

His heart was obliterated, a dead and broken thing that would never beat again. Would never feel anything again but the bottomless pain of loss.

Jacinda...

He missed her. Longed for her. The earthy scent of her. The sound of her laughter. The otherworldly silver-blue light of her hellfire. Her magic. The shape of her mouth when she said his name, when she sighed for him, when she came for him.

When she loved him.

How had it all come to this?

"Back so soon, Angel?" A voice called out from the darkness, the now-familiar form of a dimpled, purple-haired demon taking shape.

"Demetria," Gabriel breathed, unable to hide the relief in his voice. "What are you doing here?"

"Saving *your* stupid vampire ass, apparently. Why the hell aren't you topside making babies with my girl?"

"Vampires can't—"

"Figuratively speaking."

Gabriel smiled at the thought, but it didn't last.

The truth stabbed him in the heart once more.

He'd never see Jacinda again.

How the fuck was that even possible?

"So what happened?" she asked. "You fall through the portal or something? Or did she change her mind about sharing and send your fanged, fine ass back for me?"

Demetria laughed, but Gabriel said nothing. No point in it.

Demetria couldn't change what he'd done any more than Gabriel himself could.

And he didn't want to. As hopeless and lost as he felt now, he'd face a thousand eternities just like this if it meant giving Jacinda even one more *day* with her father. Whole and alive. At peace.

The demon's laughter faded, and she cocked her head, scrutinizing him. "Gabriel, seriously. I don't understand. What are you doing here? I thought… Wait. Are you… Oh *no*. Don't tell me… no. You didn't. You *absolutely* did *not* do what I think you did. Did you?"

"I… might have?"

"Are you fucking insane?"

"Certifiable."

She glared at him, black eyes gleaming with anger. "You made a demon deal."

"She was going to take her, Demetria. I had no choice."

"*She*, as in… Oh, you stupid-ass bloodsucker, you did *not* just say that. Her mother? Of all the demons in hell, you made a deal with Jacinda's *mother*?" She pressed her lips together and shook her head, her admonishment ripping open his wounds all over again. "So this is your eternity? Your fucking *eternity*?"

Eternity.

What did that even mean anymore?

Down here, every minute that passed in Jacinda's life

would feel like a decade to Gabriel. For all he knew, his body hadn't even turned to ash yet.

A sharp pain lanced his heart, and he paced the dark emptiness, picturing her holding him in the Ravenswood crypt, picturing his body turning to ash in her arms. Picturing the dust of his bones coating her porcelain skin, her lips, alighting on her dark lashes.

He wondered if she'd keep him in an urn or let him go.

Wondered if she'd gather him up and release him, or bury him beneath the earth—perhaps in the Enchanted rose gardens.

He wondered if she'd visit him there, or if she'd leave New York with her father as she'd once talked about.

So many unanswered questions, so much pain. He only just arrived, and already Gabriel felt as if he'd spent a thousand years locked in this darkness, dying a brutal new death with every beat of his heart.

"Um, Angel?" Demetria said softly. "Hate to break up your little existential crisis, but it looks like you've got company."

Gabriel stopped pacing. Lifted his head. Readied himself for another battle—the first, he was certain, of many more to come.

A dark figure emerged, lines and colors slowly sharpening, like an old photograph coming to life in a chemical bath.

The angular face. The broad shoulders. The familiar, purposeful gait.

Then the scent washed over him—the barest hint of bergamot, a whiff of cologne so faint it could only be a memory—and for a moment Gabriel forgot he was in hell.

For a moment, he was back at Ravenswood.

For a moment, he was back in his childhood home in West Sussex.

For a moment, time stopped, and the all-encompassing darkness fell away, and the wretched ache in Gabriel's heart evaporated.

He forgot about the cruelty. The betrayals. The treachery that had nearly destroyed their family from the inside out.

And all that remained, standing before him as if he'd just stepped out of a dream, was the brother he'd once so fiercely loved.

"Malcolm," he whispered, and the name felt as musty as old parchment in his mouth. "But you're… you're dead."

Malcolm cocked his head, cold eyes narrowing. "And you're *not*, if memory serves."

"*Excuse* you?" Demetria stepped between them, glaring first at Gabriel, as if he should've warned her this was coming, then at Malcolm. "You lost, bloodsucker?"

"And who the fuck might *you* be?" Malcolm asked.

"I *might* be the only friend Angel's got down here. Who the fuck might *you* be?"

"Oh, don't mind me. I'm just an allegedly dead vampire trying to determine why the *fuck* this allegedly live one is in hell." He turned his cold eyes back on Gabriel. "And you, *Angel*, have approximately eight seconds to tell me."

The emptiness in those once golden eyes was startling, finally snapping Gabriel out of his momentary shock.

He sucked in a deep breath. The memories rushed right back with it.

Malcolm, siding with their enemies against Dorian.

Malcolm, intentionally undermining the royal family.

Malcolm, punching a hole through Charlotte's torso, nearly ending her life.

"Or what?" Gabriel said. "You're going to kill me? Newsflash, brother. You're a little too late."

Malcolm laughed, a sound as vapid as his eyes.

"I'm not going to kill you," he said. Then, nodding behind Gabriel and Demetria, "But I'm pretty sure *that* bitch might."

"Come now, Malcolm," the bitch in question practically purred, the sound of her voice turning Gabriel's stomach. "Is that any way to speak about your brother's new master? We're practically family now, aren't we? Something I'm in dire need of now that one of my daughters has abandoned me and the other has gotten herself killed."

As if the loss of her precious daughters were merely an annoyance, the mother shrugged and snapped her black-tipped fingers, and all at once, the darkness fell away, revealing the scorched wasteland where he'd met her earlier.

The place where he'd signed away his eternal soul.

Gabriel blinked, his eyes adjusting to the change of scenery. Red sky choked with black clouds, just like before. Piles of smoldering bones.

And behind the mother who now owned his soul, a great maw stretched across the earth, a fathomless black abyss that glowed red in the center, pulsing like a heartbeat.

"What is she talking about?" Malcolm demanded.

Gabriel crouched down and picked up a black stone, then cast it into the pit. He waited for it to hit the bottom, but the sound never came. "She and I made a deal, Malcolm. A binding agreement."

"Worst idea ever," Demetria said, glaring at the mother with a look that could tear another hole in the veil.

The mother glared right back, her smile smug.

Through gritted teeth, Malcolm said, "And the terms?"

"I pledged my soul to her upon my death," Gabriel replied. "My death also being part of the deal, which, upon further reflection… Yes. Worst idea ever."

"Can't be overstated," Demetria said.

Gabriel nodded and stared off into the pit, mesmerized by the pulsating light. He felt the echo of it in his chest, the dull thud of a broken thing that could no longer beat on its own.

It was essentially the same deal Zachary Colburn had made. Escort Jacinda safely back to the earthly plane, and then...

"And your soul," Malcolm said. "How long, exactly, will she own it?"

"For the span of her eternal life," he replied.

"Such a sweet gesture." The mother touched her heart, her eyes sparkling. "Our little white knight, dashing in to save my daughter, sparing her the pain of imprisonment in hell. Very Romeo and Juliet. Of course, now the poor dear will have to spend her immortal life topside, which isn't exactly an upgrade, is it?"

"I would've done it to spare her even one *minute* with you," Gabriel hissed. "One. So don't talk to me about—" The words died suddenly on his tongue, his mind snagging on something the mother had said. "Wait. Immortal life? Jacinda... Jacinda's *immortal*?"

The mother clucked her tongue and shook her head as if Gabriel were the last one in on the secret.

"Are you fucking *kidding* me?" Demetria said. "She's immortal?"

Immortal? Gabriel still couldn't wrap his head around it. All this time, he never knew. *Jacinda* never knew.

They could have had an eternity together. An immortal life.

Dorian's words echoed in his memory, each one slicing through his heart like broken glass.

It's a cruel thing to be given a gift you didn't even realize you'd wanted—needed—only to have it taken from you the moment you've finally come to accept it...

"No matter," the mother said with a shrug. "She's there. You're here. Pity, really. But, as I told you before, rules are rules."

Malcolm sighed and shook his head at Gabriel as if he were the stupidest vampire who'd ever walked the earth. Then, turning to the mother, he said, "This deal. It grants you the right to claim Gabriel's soul for your *eternal* life?"

She nodded and smoothed her hands over the lapels of her pinstripe suit, preening. "I'm almost disappointed the negotiations weren't a little more challenging. A royal vampire should know better than to accept the first offer."

"Agreed." Malcolm shrugged and gazed out across the black pit, pretending to lose interest. "Oh, just one more question."

"What's that?"

"Should your eternity come to an untimely end, does that render the deal null and void?"

"Untimely end?" The mother laughed. "I'm an original, immortal demon."

Malcolm shrugged. "Rules are rules."

She opened her mouth. Closed it. Hesitated.

And in that fraction of a second, Malcolm shoved a blade right through her original, immortal eyeball.

The Blade of Azerius.

The weapon flickered, lighting up her skull as if she'd been electrocuted.

The mother didn't even have time to scream. The clothing and skin melted instantly from her bones, revealing the brittle black skeleton beneath.

Still clutching the bone handle, Malcolm yanked the blade from her eye socket.

Her bones collapsed at their feet, smoldering.

Gabriel couldn't speak. Couldn't breathe. All he could do was clutch at his skull, trying to keep his fucking brains from leaking out.

Demetria, however, was damn near dancing.

"Holy shit," she said, beaming at Malcolm. "Holy hell-in-a-handbasket, balls-of-the-devil shit. You killed her. You actually killed her."

"*What?*" Malcolm shrugged, a smooth, very un-Malcolm-like grin sliding across his face. "I didn't like the way she was looking at my brother."

Demetria laughed. "You're a funny one, Allegedly Dead. Maybe I'll let you stick around after all."

"Is that so?" Malcolm gave the woman a once-over, his gaze settling on her sparse purple hair. "I appreciate your generosity, Violet. Maybe I'll let you stick around too."

"Deal." She held out her hand to shake, but Malcolm only grinned.

"I don't think so. Unlike my brother, I *always* read the fine print."

"Can't blame a girl for trying." She feigned a huff of indignation, then said, "Fine. Since it seems you're *not* here to kill my cousin's favorite vampire, I guess I'll take off—let you two catch up."

"Demetria, wait," Gabriel said, finally finding his voice. Panic simmered inside. She'd said it herself—she was his only friend in hell. Now she wanted to leave? "No need to rush off. We've only just—"

"Sorry, Angel. I don't do other people's family drama—got enough of my own." She stretched up on her tiptoes, pressed a kiss to Gabriel's cheek. "You'd better not be here when I get back, or we're going to have words. And by words, I mean I'm *roasting* your fine ass. And no, not in the sexy, candle wax, what's-your-safe-word kind of way."

Then, with another laugh and a hard swat on his so-called fine arse, the spunky, violet-haired demon was off, leaving Gabriel to face the pile of bones and his dead brother alone.

CHAPTER TWENTY-FOUR

With quick, practiced movements, Malcolm wiped the blade clean on the bottom of his shirt, then kicked the still-smoldering bones of the mother into the abyss.

"Best not to leave a trail for anyone to follow," he explained, sitting down on a flat slab of rock at the edge of the pit to further inspect the blade. "Even in hell, someone's always watching."

Gabriel could only stare.

The Malcolm he remembered—the man he'd last seen in Bloodbath—was unhinged. A madman clinging to the vestiges of old regrets, fueled only by bitterness and revenge.

And before that—before he'd gone rogue and betrayed his entire bloodline— Malcolm had been a self-important dickhead who turned his nose up at anyone he'd deemed beneath him and doled out judgment for even the slightest breach of manners.

But *this* Malcolm… He was neither vengeful nor superior. *This* Malcolm—*hell's* Malcolm—was hard and cold, utterly devoid of passion. Stripped right down to the essentials, like a man who'd been shipped off to war as a boy and returned an old man, hollowed of his history, his memories, his dreams, devoid of all but the will to survive.

Gabriel met his brother's eyes, and the emptiness he found there terrified him more than all the demons of hell.

And yet…

Gabriel couldn't deny the surge of emotion in his heart, the spiraling ache of grief and despair that could only come from staring death in the face and knowing it'd taken something from you—some irretrievable thing whose absence would forever haunt your steps.

In a family as fraught as theirs, betrayal had the power to sever obligation. To eradicate all bonds of loyalty, duty, even of brotherhood.

But it couldn't sever love.

And now, despite everything Malcolm had broken in life, Gabriel wanted nothing more than to tell him how much he'd mourned him. Privately, wordlessly, in all the small, often imperceivable ways the heart laments the things that could've been—that *should* have been, if only someone had said the right words, done the right thing.

He wanted to tell him how much he'd missed him. How his death had left a hole in the Redthorne brotherhood not unlike the hole in Malcolm's chest—a black wound that time would never heal.

He wanted to tell him about Obsidian, how they still

kept a place for him at the VIP table—the white rose, a glass of blood, his memory as alive in death as his body had been in life, even if none of them could bring himself to say Malcolm's name out loud.

He wanted to tell him he sometimes caught a glimpse of him in his brothers' eyes, heard him in their laughter, felt his presence even in their rage, and was glad of those moments, even as they broke his heart.

He wanted to tell him he loved him.

But when he finally sat beside his brother on the rocky ledge and the acrid air burned through his lungs and all the world vanished beneath his feet in that dead, smoking hole, Gabriel could no more find the words to speak than he could the courage to meet his brother's eyes.

Instead, nodding toward the blade in Malcolm's hands, he said only, "I thought it was destroyed."

Malcolm laughed, turning it over in his hand. A bit of bone char still clung to the handle, and he rubbed it away with his thumb. "Sorry, Frodo. Not the kind of thing you simply toss into the fiery inferno from whence it came."

"It needs to be obliterated, Mac. We can't risk it falling into demon hands. Not in my realm *or* this one. Not anywhere."

"It's indestructible."

"But when I killed Azerius, everything—"

"Went nuclear. Yes, I felt it. Halfway across the realms, I felt it."

"How the fuck did you find the thing?"

"This blade is connected to me. Eternally." He lifted his

shirt, revealing a black, fist-sized wound just below his sternum, weeping with blood and infection. Tiny black fissures spiderwebbed out from the center, the skin around them blistered and cracked.

"Fucking hell," Gabriel whispered. "Tell me I didn't do that when I stabbed Azerius."

"You didn't. That was Dorian's handiwork. I felt it when you stabbed the bastard, though. Straight through the heart. You always did know how to deliver those fatal blows, brother."

Gabriel gasped. "If I'd known about the connection, I—"

"Oh, don't give me the wounded puppy eyes. It's not as bad as it looks." Malcolm quickly pulled his shirt back into place, wincing as his knuckles scraped the raw skin.

Gabriel pretended not to notice, but the pain slicing through his brother's eyes was hard to miss.

For a long moment, they sat in silence. An hour? A month? The passage of time was impossible to comprehend in hell.

Then Malcolm sighed and said, "Since you're here, there's something I want you to know."

Gabriel nodded, sensing where this was going. From the moment they'd found each other here—hell, maybe even from the moment they'd found each other back in New York, fifty years after their previous encounter—it was always leading back to this.

The betrayal. The confessions. The deep, dark river of secrets and lies that'd been running beneath the foundations of their family for centuries, slowly poisoning them.

"I would *never* betray Dorian," he said, so soft Gabriel had to lean in close to catch it. "I'd never betray any of you. Everything that happened was by design. *My* design."

He told Gabriel the story—how he'd feigned his desires for an alliance with Duchanes, pushing Dorian at every turn. How he'd embedded himself deep in enemy territory, befriending the low-level vampires that had served Chernikov and Duchanes, acting as one of them—fiendish and depraved. Criminal. How he'd pretended to despise his brothers—his blood—just to keep them safe.

"Our enemies believed our family was fractured," he continued. "That Father's death had left us all so scattered and confused, we'd never be able to claw our way back to stability, let alone power. It didn't take much acting on my part to convince them the rumors were true."

"But why convince them at all?" Gabriel asked. "We're *brothers*, Mac. Despite what Father would have us believe, we were supposed to stick together. To back Dorian as the rightful king and decide how to deal with our enemies from a position of strength and unity. All our skirmishes, all our family drama... It should've stayed within the walls of Ravenswood."

"We were outnumbered and outmaneuvered. You know that, Gabriel. Infiltrating the other camp as one of their own... It was the only way."

"You should've trusted me. I could've helped you. Together, we might've—"

"The only way to convince our enemies of my treason was to first convince my family. I *was* backing Dorian—but first, I needed to force his hand." Malcolm shook his head and sighed. "You saw him. You know what he was like after Father's death. He didn't want to be king any more than he wanted to be that monster's son."

Gabriel looked out across the pit, feeling the weight of his brother's confession—the weight of their Father's tainted legacy—deep in his bones.

"And summoning Azerius?" he asked. "Was that to force Dorian's hand as well?"

Malcolm nodded, his hand tightening on the bone handle of the blade.

"I watched you punch a hole in Charlotte's torso," Gabriel said. "You had her heart clutched in your fist, one breath—one bloody *twitch*—from turning her into ash."

"Azerius had a claim on Charlotte's soul. Dorian may have been slow to act against our political enemies, but when it came to that woman? You know as well as I—he would've stormed the very gates of hell and waged his war until every last demon was obliterated."

Gabriel could only nod.

Malcolm was right. Dorian absolutely *would've* waged that war. At the time, Gabriel had thought him as mad as Malcolm.

But now, he understood.

Gabriel nearly laughed. He'd once told Jacinda that fear made honest fools of them all, but in truth, it wasn't fear that trampled logic and reason. Wasn't fear that obliterated sanity and turned otherwise rational men into blundering

246

halfwits who believed they could take on the demons of hell and win.

It was love.

"Summoning Azerius…" Malcolm turned over the blade again, the raven's wing reflecting the deep red of the sky. "I didn't know for sure it would kill me. I'd overheard heard Dorian talking about it in the crypts with Isabelle— they hadn't even known I was there. I listened to their speculations, to the passages from Father's journals, and suddenly it was like… like a light bulb exploding in my mind. If Dorian attempted to kill his own brother with Azerius' blade, there was a good chance it'd bring the demon to our realm, where Dorian could destroy him."

"You knew Dorian would do just that," Gabriel said. "End him."

It wasn't a question.

"I told you, brother," Malcolm said. "There was never a time when I *wasn't* backing our king."

"Looking after him, just as you promised."

Mac held his gaze for a beat, a flicker of warmth igniting in the otherwise empty depths.

Nearly two hundred fifty years ago, on the night the Redthornes had been turned into vampires, their mother and youngest siblings had been slaughtered. Their mother's final words had been for Mac.

"You must look out for them, for I fear your brother's soft heart will be the death of you all…"

In service to his vow, he'd gone so deep undercover,

become so utterly unrecognizable, even the Redthornes themselves believed he'd truly turned on them.

They hadn't even held a memorial.

"I'm so sorry, Malcolm," Gabriel said now, his voice breaking. "We should have known better than to doubt you."

"I don't regret what I did. Only that I hurt you. The things I said to you, to Dorian. What I did to Charlotte…" Malcolm shook his head, gazing out across the ruined hellscape. "It's a thing for which I fear I cannot atone."

"*We're* the ones who should atone, Mac. You died for this. For us. And we—"

Malcolm's laugh rang out, sharp and bitter. "I don't know what I am now, brother, but I assure you—it wasn't Death who claimed me on that rooftop."

"Then who?"

He stared at the blade. "I've no idea."

"We know it obliterates demons. Even here in hell, it killed Azerius and the mother both."

"And it turns humans into vessels," Malcolm said. "According to the information Dorian and Isabelle had."

"Right. But you're a vampire. We didn't know how it would affect our kind." He met Malcolm's eyes again. "We *still* don't know, do we?"

"I'm here, right?"

"Are you a demon? A lost soul? Are you hellbound?"

"I don't know, Gabriel. My body is gone—ash in the wind. This is just…" Malcolm ran a hand down his torso, wincing again as he passed over his wound. "…whatever's left of my soul, I suppose. You were my brother in life, so you're seeing me as a whole person. But I'm not. Not anymore."

"You could be." New hope sparked to life in Gabriel's heart, his thoughts coming fast and furious. "Aiden was trapped here. Jacinda's father as well. We sent their souls back through the portal and—"

"I'm aware."

"We saved them, Mac. They're alive. Whole. I felt it happen the moment we reached the crypts, just before I…" Gabriel closed his eyes, swallowing the tightness in his throat. He didn't want to think about his death. About Jacinda's hands covered in ash. His life might've been over, but for Malcolm, if there was even the slightest chance… "I can send you home, Mac. I can figure out how to do the portal spell. Or find a witch here who can help. Demetria— she's a demon. Perhaps she could tap into hell's power and—"

"No, Gabriel. I've no body to return to. If you send me back now, my soul will be cursed to roam for eternity. No peace."

"And you've found peace here, have you?"

"Yes, I—"

A burst of red lightning split the sky, chased by an explosion of thunder that rattled their very bones. All around them, the air turned hotter, dryer, brimstone stinging their eyes.

Malcolm sighed. "Well, maybe not peace. Acceptance, though. I suppose there's a peace in that."

"They'll find one," Gabriel pressed. "A vessel. Not the same as the old Mac, of course, but maybe—"

"Are you trying to upgrade me, brother?" Malcolm laughed, another hint of warmth in his eyes, stoking the flames of Gabriel's hope.

"Oh, absolutely," he teased. "So if you've got any requests, now's the time."

"Bit taller, you're thinking?"

"Better hair, at the very least."

"What? What's wrong with my hair?"

"It's pretentious. Suits you, but it's pretentious."

Malcolm bristled. "If *my* hair is pretentious, yours is downright—"

Gabriel grabbed his arm, as warm and solid as it'd ever been in life. "Go *home*, Mac. To Ravenswood. To your family. Let me help you. *Please*."

Malcolm's smile faded, the warmth draining from his eyes. He turned to look out over the pit again and sighed, his shoulders slumping. "I'm not leaving here."

"Problem with that, brother," Gabriel said, "is I made a vow."

Never again…

His brother was alive. Or at least, not entirely gone. He wouldn't—couldn't leave him to rot. To burn. To lose whatever shreds of humanity were left of the man inside to this brutal, terrible place.

"I won't turn my back on you, Mac."

Malcolm shook his head. "I'm already gone, brother."

Gabriel got to his feet, and another bolt of lightning

arced across the sky, setting the black clouds on fire. The acrid air sizzled in his lungs like hellfire, making it nearly impossible to take a full breath.

This was his life now, he realized. An eternity of pain and suffering.

But it didn't have to be Mac's.

"Father's life tore us apart," Gabriel said, his voice cracking from the scorched air, from the heartache, from centuries of regrets slithering out from the darkest places of his soul. "His death brought us back together. And for the first time in fifty years, I thought maybe there was a chance we might… But then Chernikov and Duchanes betrayed us, and you… you left us, Mac. You died a traitor, an enemy. Now you're telling me that's not how it happened at all, and here you are, still breathing, still… something. Something, Mac! If Dorian knew—"

"He can *never* know. Not about what I did. Not about this place." Malcolm stood up, grabbed Gabriel's shoulder. "To you and the others, I've been gone a few months. But to me, a thousand eternities have passed. I don't expect you to understand, but…" He glanced down at the blade still gripped in his hand, then back out across the wasteland, shaking this head. "This is my life now. No home. No family. Nothing but this weapon and a lifetime of regrets keeping me warm at night."

The hope fizzled in Gabriel's heart, replaced with a new heaviness, hot and sticky. Mac was a man of many secrets, but Gabriel knew his brother well enough to know this battle was lost.

"Not entirely true," Gabriel said, attempting to find the bright side. Malcolm may have nullified the mother's contract, but Gabriel was still dead—it happened as soon as they got back to the crypts. That, too, was part of the deal, just as it had been for Jacinda's father all those years ago. "I was always bound for hell. Just happened a bit earlier than I'd planned. So yeah, best get used to this face, brother. You're stuck with me for eternity."

"As much as I'd love to wander the realms of hell with my baby brother, I'm afraid that particular threat has an expiration date of about…" Malcolm's gaze shifted to a spot behind Gabriel, then narrowed. "…soon. *Very* soon."

Gabriel spun on his heel, bracing for some new attack. A demon. Hellfire. Some new, unspeakable nightmare custom-made by his own shame and guilt, ready to welcome him to his eternal suffering.

But there, sparkling in the air before him, was a sight that stole the breath from his lungs.

Magic. Twin currents of light and dark, their silver-blue shimmer as familiar to him as the scent it'd unleashed on the air—raw earth and black pepper. Cloves and cinnamon.

"So," Malcolm said, stepping up beside him. "Mind telling me who the fuck *that* might be?"

"That," Gabriel said, his voice full of awe, "is the woman I was going to marry."

The moment the words were out, Gabriel realized they were true.

He *was* going to marry her. Was planning to spend his

life with her—a life that felt like it hadn't even existed before she'd crashed into it.

But that was all in the past now.

"A witch?" Malcolm laughed. "You fell in love with a witch? *You?* Impossible."

"Witch-demon hybrid, if we're going for accuracy."

"And necromancer. Leave it to you to omit the most interesting detail."

Gabriel shook his head. "That was a long time ago."

"Seems like she's revisiting an old hobby, then."

Gabriel lifted his hands, trailing his fingers through the silver-blue mist as if he were skimming an ocean wave. His skin tingled where the magic touched him.

Where *Jacinda* touched him.

He gasped, suddenly breathless in a way that had nothing to do with the brimstone and hellfire. "How is this… how is this possible? I died. I… I'm ash to her now."

"Not necessarily," Mac said. "Time moves in strange, unfathomable ways here. Topside? You might've only just died."

"But—"

"There's that second, Gabriel. The last heartbeat before we turn to ash." Mac touched his shoulder once more, gentle this time. Then, his voice barely a whisper, "Opportunities like this don't come around more than once. Best not miss it, brother."

Gabriel met Malcolm's eyes. Saw his own tears reflected there, a moment as fleeting as that final heartbeat before the ashes.

They said time moved more slowly in hell, but now Gabriel felt it all slipping through his fingers like water. How long had he been trapped in hell? How long had he sat on the edge of the abyss with the brother he'd long thought dead? How much time had they wasted talking about weapons and wars, the misdeeds of the past?

Now, all Gabriel wanted was more time. A minute. Just one more fucking *minute* to talk to his brother.

But Malcolm had already turned his back. Was already walking away, no goodbyes, no explanations, just as he had in life.

Gabriel blinked once more, and Malcolm was gone, nothing more than footprints in the ash.

A hot wind blew across the wasteland, erasing them as if Malcolm had never been there at all.

The sky flashed, one bolt then another, thunder making the ground tremble beneath him. Fire rained down, sizzling on the ground, eating up all the air.

Gabriel tilted his head toward the sky, fire and blood and brimstone, the end of all things, and closed his eyes. In every flash of lightning, he saw his demons.

Augustus Redthorne waiting for him in the stables, boots awash in the blood of the blind, deaf goat Gabriel had loved.

Be merciless, Gabriel Redthorne, or you will find yourself at the mercy…

The witch he'd murdered in the woods.

I can't help you, vampire. Accept your fate and embrace your immortality…

The demons he'd tortured, the vampires, the rivers upon rivers of blood he'd spilled. Consumed.

The secrets he'd kept. The lies. The brothers he'd disappointed, pushed away, failed, pushed away again.

And finally, the child, blood streaking her face, dark eyes full of accusation. Pain. Loss.

"I'm sorry," he whispered. Tears spilled unbidden, sliding into his mouth, hot and salty. "I'm so, so sorry."

He felt the touch of her tiny hands on his cheeks. Her sour breath on his face. Her tangled hair blowing into his mouth. And he knew it would be the last time he'd ever see her.

"Wake up, vampire prince," she whispered. "It's time for you to leave."

Another shock of lightning, a hot breath sucked into aching lungs, and Jacinda's magic surged around him, a pull he couldn't resist. *Wouldn't* resist.

"Moonflower," Gabriel whispered, the name caressing his lips like a promise. A vow.

And in that breathless, beautiful moment, the witch-demon hybrid he was going to marry reached deep inside him, grabbed onto his soul, and snatched him back from the depths of hell.

CHAPTER TWENTY-FIVE

One Week Later

New Year's Eve.

For most people, it was a night of reckoning. A time for reflecting on the past and embracing the hope and promise of a fresh start.

Not so for Gabriel Redthorne.

For the last fifty years, while the denizens of Las Vegas donned their finery and waited in lines for hours just to get into one of his club's infamous parties, Gabriel had spent the passage from one year to the next alone in the desert, as far away from the press of humanity as he could get without leaving the city limits.

And while he lay beneath a moonless sky wondering how much longer his immortal doom would truly last, his patrons danced and gambled, swallowed his designer pills and top-shelf booze, flitted from one fling to the next, all the while promising their gods and devils both that next year would be better—that *anything* would be better than the year they'd just suffered through.

For that one night each year, they truly believed in magic.

And Gabriel, who'd never believed in magic and had long since run out of hope, hated them for it.

But now, just before midnight on the last day of another year, he was beginning to see the holiday through different eyes.

Through the eyes of a vampire who'd spent far too long living in the shadows of his past, chained by his own guilt.

Though the eyes of a vampire who'd fallen in love with a witch-demon hybrid who'd shown him that second chances didn't just come on one magical night at the stroke of midnight each year, but on *every* night, in *every* moment —so long as you had the courage and grace to ask for them.

Standing on the balcony overlooking the packed main floor of Obsidian, Gabriel sipped his bourbon, appreciating *this* moment. Appreciating all the second chances he'd finally welcomed into his heart.

Downstairs, it seemed as if the whole of New York's supernatural elite had turned out, all of them laughing and dancing, drinking, counting down the final hours of the year.

Across the crowd, gathered around their VIP table, his brothers traded toasts and stories, celebrating their liberation from the curse that'd damned their bloodline for centuries. Isabelle and Cole were there too, as well as Sasha, tucked in close to Aiden, who was still recovering from his ordeal in hell.

He hadn't wanted to talk about what he'd seen there, what the Hall of Broken Mirrors had shown him. And though he'd put on his bravest face, hiding behind his usual snark and humor, every now and then Gabriel would meet Aiden's gaze, and a darkness would slither into his eyes, and Gabriel's heart would stutter in his chest, terrified that the ordeal had done something irreparable.

But, like so many things in the complicated history of the Redthorne royal vampires, the story of Aiden's journey to hell was a thing best left undisturbed.

Just like the story of Malcolm's journey.

Gabriel lifted the bourbon to his lips again, catching sight of the untouched glass of blood and the white rose his family had set at the end of the table for their fallen brother, as they always did.

In the week since his return from hell, he'd wanted so badly to tell Dorian about finding Malcolm. About the confessions he'd shared. About how much he'd changed. About the fact that he even existed at all—not quite dead, not quite lost, but somewhere in between, trapped in a place where nothing but a *shred* of hope still lingered.

But hope—even the barest shred of it—felt too much like a promise. And after everything Malcolm had said about not wanting to leave hell, Gabriel wasn't ready to make that promise to the rest of his brothers just yet.

Not until he figured out a way to keep it.

But Jacinda? She knew. For Gabriel and his witch-demon, there were no more secrets but the ones they kept together. They were partners in every way, just as they'd promised each other—a vow more sacred than any he'd made before or since.

And with Jace at his side, Gabriel knew he'd figure out how to bring Malcolm back. How to make his family whole again—the brothers bound to him by blood as well as the people bound to him by love. For Gabriel, there was no longer a difference.

"I think my New Year's Eve date is trying to ditch me," a soft, sexy voice whispered against his neck. The scent of earth and black pepper drifted through the air. "Don't suppose you'd like to fill in?"

Gabriel laughed, and at the press of her lips on his cheek, something warmed inside him.

Ah, there it was again.

Hope.

How long had he lived without it? How many decades had he lived in darkness, sleepwalking from one night to the next?

Never again.

He turned to face his woman, running a hand down to her hip.

She wore a short satin dress that clung to every curve, as black as obsidian, her hair twisted into an elegant braid that wrapped around her head like a silver crown, showing off her bare neck and shoulders.

Her lush red smile was all for him.

"You look…" Gabriel marveled at the sight, his heart kicking his ribs, his cock stirring.

He couldn't find the word. Didn't even bother to try. It didn't exist.

"It's almost midnight," Jacinda said, her eyes sparkling. "I was hoping to find someone to kiss."

"*Someone?* No particular qualifications?"

"Hmm. I'd like him to be cute, of course. Well-dressed. Maybe a little mouthy." She leaned in close. "Know anyone who might be available?"

He traced his thumb along her jaw, down to her collarbone, skimming the top edge of her breasts. "I think I might."

"Does this mean you're going to kiss me, Gabriel Redthorne?" she whispered.

"Oh, I'm *absolutely* going to kiss you, little moonflower. But not yet. And not here." He held out his arm. "Fancy a walk?"

They headed downstairs and out onto St. Mark's Place, the night crisp and cool, a light snow dusting the tops of the buildings that surrounded them.

Gabriel removed his suit jacket and draped it over her shoulders, and she leaned in closer, letting out a soft sigh of contentment.

They hadn't had much time alone since they'd been back—Gabriel wanted to give her time with her father, who was still acclimating to his return. He'd been staying in Dorian's guest house while he and Jacinda looked for a new place for him upstate. As an earth mage who'd been denied access to actual earth for a quarter-century, the man had no interest in living in the city now.

As far as Gabriel knew, he'd only been back to Manhattan once since his return from hell—to take his daughter to Rockefeller Center.

Gabriel was grateful they'd been able to save him. With her mother and sister gone and her father returned to her, Jacinda had never been so happy. So at peace.

But now, he took a moment to appreciate the fact that they were alone, enjoying a few quiet moments outside before the clock struck twelve.

"Gabriel," she whispered, and the sudden urgency in her voice made him stop.

"I have something to say to you," she continued, "but every time I try to figure out how, the words get all tangled up. I feel like I should apologize, but the fact that you're even standing here…" She shook her head. "I can't. I'm not sorry."

He cupped her face. "Not sorry for what, love?"

"It's just…" She pressed her lips together. Shook her head. Sighed. "You *died* that night, Prince. You were seconds away from turning to ash. I know how you feel about resurrection, but I didn't know what else to do. I felt your soul leaving your body, and I just… I couldn't let you go."

"Jacinda—"

"Honestly, I had no idea if I could even resurrect a vampire who wasn't a gray. Especially without an amulet."

"Jace—"

"I just knew I had about three seconds before you turned into ash and I couldn't bear it and I—"

"*Jacinda.*"

She closed her mouth and lowered her eyes, shame coloring her cheeks.

And Gabriel knew, all at once, where this was coming from.

In this *city, witch, death is a kindness. That you'd seek to defy it is nothing less than madness…*

His old words echoed, and Gabriel tucked a finger under her chin, tipping her face up to look at him once more.

"*Love* is the kindness, Jace," he said softly. "And I have never been so bloody ecstatic to have been so bloody wrong in all my life."

She finally smiled, her eyes filling with relief. "So you're not mad I brought you back?"

Gabriel shook his head. The fact that she could even *think* that… That she'd honestly believe he wasn't ready to drop to the ground and kiss her feet in thanks for saving his life…

"Come with me," he said suddenly.

Without waiting for a reply, he swept her into his arms and blurred her up to the rooftop above his penthouse.

"What… what is this?" she whispered, her mouth wide with surprise as she got her bearings and took in the sight.

Beneath a new, climate-controlled glass encasement, the entire rooftop had been exquisitely landscaped. A patch of wild mint here, a tangle of moonflowers there, rows upon rows of herbs and plants—everything he'd seen her use in her spells and concoctions, everything he'd ever heard her mention with so much as a passing word.

"This is your home now, Jacinda," he said, hands on her shoulders. "*Our* home. You deserve all the things that make you happy. I want to give them to you—tonight and always."

Jacinda stared out across the expanse, not speaking. Barely even breathing.

"If you don't love it," Gabriel went on, "we can leave the city, of course. Find something upstate near your father, or… I don't know. Another state altogether, if that's what you want. Anything, love. Just say the word, and it's yours. Ours. Home, I mean. Wherever you want it to be."

She finally turned to face him again, her eyes glittering with tears.

"Home," she said softly. "For so long, I thought I would only ever belong in hell."

"And now?"

"If home is a place, Gabriel, then it's this one right here." She pressed her hand to his heart, her bright-red smile lighting him up all over again. "And there's nowhere else I'd rather be. Well, except for maybe…"

He leaned in close. Brushed his mouth along the shell of her ear. "Maybe *what*?"

"Are those rose bushes?" she asked, gesturing to the back corner of the encasement.

"They are indeed."

With another wicked grin that made him instantly hard, she took his hand and led him into the thicket.

Together they knelt in the dirt, and tonight—a night for new beginnings—Gabriel allowed his woman to take charge.

She pushed him onto his back and climbed on top, straddling him.

He realized, in that most blissful fucking moment, the witch wasn't wearing panties.

A soft moan escaped his lips, and he pushed her dress up to her waist, relishing in the feel of her bare heat against his cock.

"I used to think my curse had to do with demon magic," he teased, "but now I know the real curse was far more treacherous."

Jacinda laughed, the movement sending shockwaves of pleasure straight to his balls. "Oh yeah? And what's the real curse, then?"

He tucked a silver-blonde curl behind her ear and smiled at the marvel of it. Of her.

In a dark whisper, he said, "I was cursed, witch-demon, to fall in love with the enemy."

"Oh, is that what I am?" She laughed, the sound of it echoing across their enchanted gardens. "Your enemy?"

"I recall asking you that very question not so long ago."

"Yes, and what did I tell you?"

"You didn't respond. You were too bloody terrified."

"Ha!" She leaned forward, sliding her palms up his

chest, slowly working his shirt buttons loose. "I think *you* were the terrified one."

"Guilty. And never has that been more true than it is in this moment." He grabbed her hands, pressed them to his lips. Inhaled the scent of her skin. Memorized the look in her eyes, the feel of her body, warm and perfect on top of him.

"Don't be afraid, Prince," she teased, slipping her hands free and reaching between her legs for the button and zipper on his pants. She fisted his cock and shifted her hips, settling on top of him once more, slowly guiding him inside.

With a deep growl, he slid his hands into her hair, freeing it from the braid, desperate to feel it loose and wild in his hands. In his mouth. Trailing over his bare torso as she bent over him, shuddering with pleasure.

"Does this feel like enemies?" she whispered, leaning forward to kiss his jaw, arching her hips, sliding up along his cock, then back down, taking him in deeper.

"No," he whispered. "That's… bloody perfect."

"How about this?" Another kiss, this time on his throat, then his collarbone, her fingernails trailing down his chest. She moved slowly, sealing a promise of pleasure with every soft, seductive arch of her hips.

She ran her tongue along his lower lip, then bit, fisting his hair and claiming his mouth with a kiss that ricocheted through his entire body.

When she spoke again, her voice was smoky. "Does *this* feel like enemies, Prince?"

"It feels like… Jacinda, it…" He gripped her hips, forcing her to stop moving, just for a moment. "It feels like I love you," he said, suddenly overcome by the force of it. Love. So much it felt as if his heart might burst if he didn't finally make his confession—one he'd been holding in all week. "I said a thing in hell, Jace. To Mac."

Her eyes widened.

"When you started the resurrection spell," he said, "we felt it. Your magic. He asked me what it was."

"And did you tell him the truth?" She flashed another grin. "That it was your enemy, come to deliver you from evil?"

Gabriel shook his head, wondering if she could feel the wild banging of his heart. "I told him it was the woman I was going to marry."

Jacinda gasped, her pulse kicking up, thighs clenching tight around him.

"So the way I see it, you've got two choices, little moon-flower." He released her hips and reached for her face, pulling her down on top of him once more. "Tell me to stop," he whispered against her mouth. "Or let me spend the rest of our immortal eternity filling your life with as much magic as you've brought into mine. Marry me, Jacinda Colburn."

Her eyes glazed with tears, and another bout of laughter burst from deep inside her.

"Bloody hell, woman," he said. "Are you going to say yes, or are you going to torture me?"

"That depends, Prince." She nipped at his lower lip

again, a new challenge flashing in her eyes. "Am I still your enemy?"

Gabriel was more than ready to flip her onto her back, claim her in the dirt, and prove to her just how *not* enemies they truly were.

But before he could say another word, the sky exploded with fireworks.

"It's midnight," he said. "I suppose you'll be wanting that kiss."

"Yes."

"Yes, you want a kiss?"

"No. I mean, yes. Yes, I want a kiss, and yes I'll marry you. I mean… I'm saying *yes*, Prince. To all of it. Yes!" She laughed again, and when she smiled at him with a light that rivaled the fireworks in the sky, it cracked him wide open, setting him on fire from the inside out.

Gabriel didn't fight it. He welcomed it. Needed it.

He slid his arms around her and finally flipped her so he was on top, his urge to claim her too overpowering to ignore. He thrust deep between her bare thighs, owning her as he always did, hot and hard and perfect, the rose bushes shuddering around them, a hundred white petals falling like the softest rain.

And when the fireworks had finally faded into trails of white smoke, and the revelers poured out of the bars and into the streets, and she fisted his hair and her body clenched tight around him, he came in a blinding hot rush, and Jacinda trembled and gasped, whispering his name to the stars as if she were writing their story upon each one, and for the first time in his long immortal life, Gabriel spoke the words of the season and deeply, truly meant them.

"Happy New Year, little moonflower. Happy New Year."

~

Thank you so much for reading Gabriel and Jacinda's epic love story!

Ahh, nothing like a broody vampire and a sassy witch to bring the heat *and* the magic. Gabriel and Jacinda's story has come to a close, but don't worry—there's still more to come in the Vampire Royals of New York world!

Don't miss a new release! Sign up for my newsletter at sarahpiperbooks.com/readers-club and I'll let you know the moment we've got more news from the Vampire Royals of New York... and any other sexy, supernatural book news you won't want to miss!

~

Vampire lovers! If you loved reading this story as much as I loved writing it, please help a girl out and **leave a review on Amazon!** Even a quick sentence or two about your favorite part can help other readers discover the book, and that makes me super happy!

If you really, *really* loved it, come hang out with me and the other amazing Vampire Royals of New York fans in our private Facebook group, Sarah Piper's Sassy Witches. Pop in for sneak peeks, cover reveals, exclusive giveaways, book chats, and plenty of complete randomness! We'd love to see you there.

XOXO
Sarah

~

Have you read Dorian and Charlotte's epic love story yet?

Catch up on the original VRNY series, starting with book one, **Dark Deception!**

~

Need even *more* hot British vampires?

I've got another spicy supernatural romance series ready to heat up your Kindle! The Witch's Rebels is a complete series about a witch outrunning her past, five smoldering-hot supernatural guardians (including the sexy, commanding alpha vampire Darius Beaumont), and the dark secret that could destroy them all.

Read on for a taste of book one, **Shadow Kissed!**

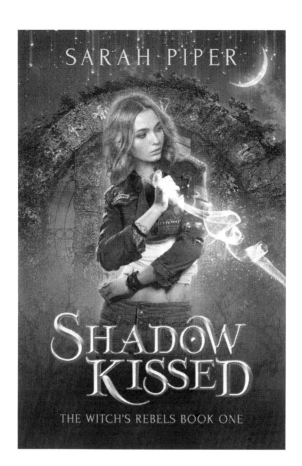

SARAH PIPER

SHADOW KISSED

THE WITCH'S REBELS BOOK ONE

Back at the scene of the crime, blood stained the alley, a sick reminder that I hadn't imagined the fight. The sound of her head hitting the pavement echoed in my memory.

"Miss Desario. I might have guessed you had something to do with this."

I jumped at the voice, though I recognized the delicious British accent immediately.

Slowly I turned to face him, tightly gripping my wooden stake.

Darius Beaumont was beautiful. Elegant, tall, and lean, he was dressed in an impeccably tailored black suit that probably cost more than I made in a year. Wavy, chin-length brown hair and a perfectly stubbled jaw stood out starkly against a crisp white dress shirt, the top two buttons undone.

His golden-honey eyes sparked with possibility.

Or hunger.

Dangerous? You bet. But good God, he was sexy. The liquid caress of his voice, the intensity in his eyes, the sheer power locked away in those lean muscles…

In a blur of movement, he tore the stake from my hand

and threw it against the bricks so hard it splintered into dozens of useless pieces.

"Now that we've taken care of that nasty business," he said calmly, "care to explain the rest?"

I lowered my eyes in a sign of respect, but I didn't back away or bow or submit to him in any way. Technically, vampires weren't allowed to feed on us without consent, but the Council tended to look the other way for all but the most heinous infractions. My policy with vamps was simple: don't give them a reason to infract.

"Explain?" I asked.

"Your involvement in this." He stepped toward me, looming so close that if he were human, I would've felt his breath on my cheeks. His imposing shadow fell across my face, making me blink as I met his gaze.

Despite the fact that he could end my life with a single touch, everything about him made my mouth water—one of the many reasons I usually avoided him.

"What makes you think I was involved?" I asked.

"Just after closing this morning, I emerged to find my delivery abandoned here and an alley full of human blood. Your scent was..." Darius picked up a lock of my hair and pressed it to his lips, closing his eyes. "Everywhere."

He knows my scent?

A shiver crept down my back, but I couldn't tell whether the idea was terrifying... or a complete turn-on. "Yeah, I... Sorry about your delivery. I got... distracted."

"I see." Darius released my hair. With a light, cool touch,

he traced my bruised cheekbone, his eyes dimming. "And this… *distraction*. Was he responsible for this?"

God, I love the way he's touching me…

The erotic caress of a vampire was a dangerous lure. Witches could defend against the power of mental influence vamps used on humans, but it took a lot of energy—something I was running severely low on. And the longer I stared at his mouth, at the way his lips curved at the edges, hinting at a soft smile behind his cool exterior, the more I wanted to give in.

But that was a *terrible* idea.

"To be fair," I said, dragging my gaze away from his lips, "you should see the other guy."

"I suppose that's his blood all over my alley?"

I nodded, toeing the pavement with my boot. "His teeth are around here somewhere, too. Unless he came back for them."

A cool smirk slid across his face. "Quite the little brawler, aren't you?"

I shrugged and forced a confident smile. "Well, nice seeing you again, Mr. Beaumont. I should probably let you get back to your guests."

"Probably." Darius's fingers trailed down from my face to my neck, his touch turning icy as it slid over my pulse points. "Is that all you have to say on the matter, then?"

I nodded, hoping he couldn't sense the tremble inside me.

"Lying to me is unwise, necromancer."

Necromancer…

More than his dangerous touch, the word made me stiffen. Every hair on my neck stood on end.

"Excluding you," he said calmly, his smile vanishing, "two humans bled in my alley this morning. One of them died. Moments later, I sensed her rise. Explain."

My heart sunk.

My so-called logical theory was falling apart. Vampires could sense human life force—it's how they figured out who was worth eating, and who had already gone cold. So if he sensed Bean die, and then rise…

You did this to me, witch…

"You're right—there's more," I admitted. "I… I can't explain it. I don't know…" Tears pricked my eyes. In a whisper only a vampire could hear, I said, "Nothing like that ever happened before. I swear. I—"

"*Miss Desario.*" The warning tone in Darius's voice stopped me cold. I swallowed hard and met his gaze, realizing how weak I must look. Like a scared little girl. Like prey.

His eyes blazed suddenly with red-hot desire. If Darius had been a younger vampire, one with less control over his predatory instincts, I'd already be dead.

He wanted me to know it. And he was giving me about five seconds to do something about it.

I hated the bullshit power games, but not as much as I'd hate being dead.

With all the confidence I could muster, I gritted my teeth, jerking free of his hold. "Message received, *vampire*. Back off."

After a beat, Darius stepped backward and turned away from me, putting some much-needed distance between my throat and his fangs.

Get your shit together, Desario.

Standing up straight again, I took a deep breath and forced the tremble out of my limbs. Scared and snackable? Definitely not a good look for me.

"Does the coven know about your… extracurricular activities?" Darius asked, still facing the wall.

As if I'd tell those witches anything.

"No one knows. *I* didn't even know I had that kind of juice until last night."

"Juice?" At this he turned around, his eyes still smoldering but slightly less terrifying. "If that was witchcraft, it's not a magic I've ever encountered among your people."

So I'm not just any old freak. I'm a super *freak! Awesome.*

"Okay, let's assume you're right," I said, clinging to the possibility that the darkness hadn't come from me after all. "If it wasn't my witchcraft, what was it?"

"Now *that* is the question, yes?" Darius considered me, his lips twisting into a calculating smile. I could practically hear the gears turning in his head, all the possibilities playing out in his hyper-logical mind. "A witch with a new toy. Imagine if you also had my strength? Speed? Immortality? Ah, the things we could achieve."

Even if I wanted to be an immortal, superstrong bloodsucker—and that was a big if—I wouldn't take the risk.

Witches were biologically human, so turning us vamp required the usual blood swap—he'd drink mine, I'd drink his. But we also had the added complication of magic in our blood, whether we used it or not. Unfortunately, no one knew how vampire blood affected us in the long term.

Because in the short term? No witch had ever survived the change.

"Perhaps we can come to an arrangement," Darius said.

"Thank you for the invitation, but that's a hard pass."

"Regardless…" The hunger in his voice sounded especially menacing out here in the alley, where no one was around to hear me scream. "The invitation remains."

"Noted."

"Come." Darius opened the door to the service entrance and gestured for me to enter ahead of him. "It seems we have some things to discuss."

I took a step backward and raised my hands. "Again, thanks for the invitation, but I—"

"Apologies for giving you the wrong impression, love." Darius clamped a hand over my shoulder, eyes blazing once again. "But *that* was not an invitation."

For creatures of the night, October in the Pacific Northwest usually meant shorter days and more time outdoors. Yet an hour after sunset, Black Ruby was already packed with vampires.

The windowless club was an elevator ride two stories down from street level, dimly lit and cool as a cave. With its exposed brick interior, wooden booths, and mahogany bar, it felt less like a sleek vampire hangout and more like a friendly neighborhood pub—though in my opinion, the things that went on here were anything but friendly.

Sitting on a high-backed stool at the bar, I scoped out the room. Most of the fang-bangers were huddled in dark booths with their blood slaves—some so pale and emaciated it was hard to tell if they were still human. The whole scene turned my stomach, but it wasn't surprising. The port city of Blackmoon Bay was a hub for runaways and transients—easy pickings for the powerful vamps.

Hell, I'd been there myself. Guess it was just dumb luck that when I'd washed up on these shores at eighteen, barely alive after two years on the run, I'd managed to avoid the vamp welcoming committee.

I'd gotten Ronan instead.

Calla would've called that a far worse fate, but then, she'd never trusted demons.

Darius set a cocktail napkin on the bar in front of me, bringing my attention back to the present. "Allow me to buy you a drink."

"Is that an invitation or a demand?"

Darius's golden eyes glinted with amusement. "That depends on whether you'll tell me what you'd like, or force me to choose for you."

I leaned forward across the bar and lowered my voice. "What exactly are we discussing tonight, Mr. Beaumont?"

"Darius. I insist."

"Yeah, I'm starting to realize that's a thing with you, *Darius*."

His eyebrow quirked, but the vampire didn't answer my question—just grabbed a glass from the rack above the bar and poured me a straight shot of Jameson.

He was making me sweat. Fine. As long as he didn't make me bleed, I could wait him out.

I downed the drink, enjoying the burn.

Darius poured me another, then glanced toward the entrance, where a group of particularly menacing vampires had just emerged from the elevator. *Rich* menacing vampires.

He cursed under his breath.

"Problem?" I asked.

"Only in keeping my schedule sorted. If you'll excuse me a moment, I've got a meeting."

"Don't let me stop you."

"I won't be more than twenty minutes." Darius shot me a warning glare. "Don't leave, Gray."

I wasn't sure I had a choice.

"Fine. But if you're not back in twenty, I'm out." I shrugged and left him to it, nursing my second drink and trying to gather my thoughts.

Damn. The vamp had something on me now. Something major. Not that he'd use it—around here, the freaks might not like each other, but we damn well kept each other's secrets. Our survival depended on it. Whether it was human cops poking too closely around our haunts or outside supernaturals looking to take over new territory, none of us wanted to bring scrutiny to the Bay.

Still... I didn't like the fact that knowledge about what

I'd done was out there. Vampires were immortal, but that didn't mean they couldn't be tortured.

Everyone had a breaking point, and everyone had a price.

"Hello, sexy."

I turned toward the smarmy voice just as the vamp it belonged to slithered onto the chair on my right. A muscle-bound blond with a nasty scar cutting down his cheek, he eyed me with obvious hunger, making my skin crawl.

I opened my mouth to tell him I was with someone else —*anyone* else—when a second vamp took the chair on my left. This one was a skinny, emo-looking dude with greasy black hair and way too many facial piercings.

Scarface wrapped a hand around my thigh and leaned in close. "I've never tasted witch before."

His gray eyes glinted with ice, colder and more deadly than the eyes of any vamp I'd ever tangled with. It was a struggle not to cower or turn away, but showing weakness now would activate his predatory instincts faster than an outright threat.

Darius was nowhere in sight.

I was stuck.

"How about joining us for a little fun tonight?" Emo asked.

"You'll like it," Scarface said.

"No thanks," I said, calm but firm. "I'm waiting for someone."

"Well, I guess that dude's gonna have to learn to live with disappointment." Scarface grabbed my arm, forcing me out of the chair. "Remember where you are and don't make a fuckin' scene."

Emo vamp closed in on my other side, digging his fingers into the flesh on my upper arm.

Panic surged, my mouth going dry. Where the hell was Darius? And worse—what if this was totally acceptable behavior at Black Ruby? Letting the customers get a little carryout for the road?

My skin prickled, and low in my belly, something dark and strange sparked to life. Ignited. Burned.

Don't let them take you, a voice inside me warned. *Kill them…*

"Let me go." I tried to jerk free, but even with the magic roiling inside me, I wasn't strong enough—especially now that Darius had destroyed my stake.

"Shut up." Emo clamped a hand around my neck, squeezing so hard it was a struggle to breathe. They dragged me away from the bar and into the back of the club, shoving me down a dimly lit hallway of what looked to be offices and storage rooms. But halfway down, Darius stepped out from behind one of the doors, his eyes blazing.

Clearly, carryout was not Black Ruby policy.

I'd never been so happy to see a vampire in my life.

"Out of the way, Beaumont," Scarface said with a sneer. "This bitch is—"

"Not on the menu, Mr. Hollis." Darius stepped into the fray and pushed me behind him, blocking me from their reach. Emo backed off immediately, but Scarface—Hollis—let out a low growl, the air around him crackling with electric tension. He and Darius were about the same height, but while Darius was lean and lithe, Hollis was a tank.

Still, my money was on the Brit.

"Are you alright, Miss Desario?" Darius asked over his shoulder, not taking his eyes off Hollis and Emo.

"I'm fine," I said. My arm muscles throbbed from the rough handling, and my neck would definitely be sporting finger-shaped bruises tomorrow, but I was still in one piece.

"Your little pet could use a lesson in manners," Hollis said. "Teasing us like she did." His threatening glare sent a chill down my spine.

God, I really hoped I'd never meet *him* alone in a dark alley. Something told me he wouldn't soon forget the witch who'd refused his so-called invitation.

Darius continued to stare him down, the picture of grace and elegance. Despite his cool demeanor, raw power emanated from his body, sending a different kind of chill down my spine.

"I presume Miss Desario has not given her consent to this arrangement," he said. "Continuing on your present course could place you in a precarious legal position, could it not?"

"This is bullshit," Emo said.

"If you'd like another opinion, Mr. Weston," Darius said, "I'd be happy to place a call to the Council and let them sort it out."

I wasn't sure what kind of legal trouble they could possibly get into—everyone knew the Council wouldn't bother with something as trivial as vamps taking a witch for their blood slave, even if it *was* against the rules. But Black Ruby was Darius's club, the warehouse district Darius's territory. Council or not, he had every right to intervene.

"I'm outta here." Emo shook his head, slinking off toward a stairwell exit at the end of the hall. "You're on your own with this bitch, Hollis."

"Excellent. Now that we've got that sorted..." Darius stepped back and took my hand, standing right at my side as he glared at the remaining vampire, the challenge in his eyes as terrifying as it was thrilling.

I sucked in a breath. I wasn't totally up on vampire hierarchies and politics, but I was pretty sure Darius's actions indicated that I was under his protection. If that were true, no other vamp could touch me without serious consequences.

Judging from the new fury flickering in Hollis's eyes, my assessment was correct.

"You sure you want to do this, *brother*?" Hollis asked.

"It's already done."

"Since when do you side with witch whores?"

Anger flared in Darius's eyes, but other than a slight tick in his jaw and a quick squeeze of my hand, he didn't move a muscle. He remained stone-cold silent for so long I was beginning to think he might just implode.

But then he raised his chin, his coiled muscles emanating raw power as he stared Hollis down. "I'm not your brother, vampire. You'd be wise to remember that."

"Oh, I will." With no move left to play, Hollis pushed

past us, knocking against my shoulder on his way out. Pinning me for just a moment with that icy, terrifying stare, he leaned in close and whispered, "I remember *everything*."

Ready for more? Dive into the sexy supernatural world of The Witch's Rebels! **Grab your copy of Shadow Kissed now!**

A New Way to Get Your Audio Fix...

Audiobook lovers, you can now buy audiobooks directly from my author store at **SarahPiperBooks.com/shop** for early access and huge savings!

The books will still be available on other retailers like Audible and Apple, but buying direct means you can:

• **Save big.** Author store prices are 30-60% off retail prices.

• **Be the first to listen.** All new releases will be available for direct buy for a limited-time advanced release 2-4 weeks before they hit Audible and Apple. After that, they'll be removed from the author store to comply with Audible's exclusivity rules for 90 days before popping up in the author store again.

• **Directly support your favorite authors and narrators.** Your support means the world to me, and helps ensure I can continue to partner with the best narrators in the industry to bring these stories to life!

Visit SarahPiperBooks.com/shop to get started!

ABOUT SARAH PIPER

Sarah Piper is a Kindle All-Star winning urban fantasy and paranormal romance author. Through her signature brew of dark magic, heart-pounding suspense, and steamy romance, Sarah promises a sexy, supernatural escape into a world where the magic is real, the monsters are sinfully hot, and the witches always get their magically-ever-afters.

Her recent works include the newly released Vampire Royals of New York series, the Tarot Academy series, and The Witch's Rebels, a fan-favorite reverse harem urban fantasy series readers have dubbed "super sexy," "imaginative and original," "off-the-walls good," and "delightfully wicked in the best ways," a quote Sarah hopes will appear on her tombstone.

Originally from New York, Sarah now makes her home in northern Colorado with her husband (though that changes frequently) (the location, not the husband), where she spends her days sleeping like a vampire and her nights writing books, casting spells, gazing at the moon, playing with her ever-expanding collection of Tarot cards, binge-watching Supernatural (Team Dean!), and obsessing over the best way to brew a cup of tea.

You can find her online at SarahPiperBooks.com and in her Facebook readers group, Sarah Piper's Sassy Witches! If you're sassy, or if you need a little *more* sass in your life, or if you need more Dean Winchester gifs in your life (who doesn't?), come hang out!

.

Printed in Great Britain
by Amazon